The Waiting

Dipavali Sen

Published By
Invincible Publishers

Published by
Invincible Publishers
201A, SAS Tower, Sector 38, Gurugram – 122003
Phone: +91-124-4034247, +91 9355675555
www.i-publish.in

First Published in 2020

ISBN: 978-81-945481-5-7

In the memory of

Shri Jyotish Chandra Roy,
freedom fighter and author,

my Dadua who introduced me to
stories of mystery and adventure.

Acknowledgment

Sincere thanks to the staff of Invincible Publishers, for the enthusiasm, enterprise, and commitment they have shown in bringing this book out in the midst of an international crisis.

I also express indebtedness to the many books, stories, films, exhibitions, and museums that have enriched me on the subject since my childhood. I thank my sons for bringing me up on dinosaur toys, science fiction and computer apps. I would also like to state here that no doubt or disrespect has been meant here for any individual or group, or any body of thought and practice, any organisation or institution. My respects to all!

Contents

Prologue: Waiting To Hatch

The egg was waiting to hatch.

It was 65 million years ago in the Pranhita-Godavari Valley of the Deccan plateau of India, then teeming with dinosaurs.

A Sauropod Dinosaur was sitting in her nest–a shallow hole in the muddy river-valley. She was laying eggs, soft and cream-coloured, shaped like ellipsoids. There were other nests too – with other dinosaur couples stomping around the swamp full of palms and ferns, the only vegetation of those times. Young ones were straying here and there and moving back to their mothers.

Suddenly, there was a searing beam of light from the clouds. A massive grey chunk came hurtling down and hit the valley with a deafening explosion.

It was a meteorite about 10 kilometres in diameter. It created a 200-kilometre crater and deposited iridium all across the valley.

The dinosaurs found the earth shaking under their legs. Somewhere far away, a volcano erupted and molten lava covered them up even as they tried to escape. Soon, the entire valley disappeared under a sheet of lava.

More upheavals – more quakes – and it moved down into the depths of the earth.

The dinosaurs went down with the rest of the valley. So did their nests full of un-hatched eggs.

One of them wondered, “Oh, what is happening outside?” It then said to itself, “Well, I will know soon enough. I just have to wait.”

Anit in Gurgaon

"Oh, for some magic to take care of those bullies!" said Anit loudly as he wiped the tears trickling out of his eyes. He trudged home, feeling the entire weight of his schoolbag upon his back.

Anit had thick, curly hair, a flat nose, and uneven teeth. His family had just shifted from Noida to Gurgaon and he had got admission to Class Six of New Gurgaon Public School. It was an old school, earlier in the older parts of Gurgaon. But now, it had shifted to a new location along Sohna Road, not too far by bus from the locality where Anit stayed. It was an impressive red-brick building with every facility for studies and sports. But the ragging he was facing as a new student at school was wearing him down.

When his parents had got their own flat in Gurgaon, Anit had been as thrilled as they had been. They had booked it some years back and visited it occasionally from Noida, where they were then staying. Thus, Anit had watched his new home at various stages of its construction and had gone through various stages of admission to the new school. He had been ready for the shift but was taken aback by the tough ragging his new class-mates were subjecting him to.

"*Yaar* Anit! Tell us how to grow such a fine tail!" Someone one would say, and Anit would give a start and half-turn to find a belt emerging from a loop at the back of his shorts.

"Anit! What a pretty printed shirt you have got!" Another would be slapping him on the back with inky palms. These were the milder forms of ragging. Anit had to bear with sudden kicks at the back and pricks from sharpened pencils. The worst among them were Sumant and Kireet, two big, burly fellows.

Anit tried telling his parents.

"You are in Class Six now," Baba said sternly. "Be a man!"

"Oh, Anit, within a year you will be making friends with them and having them over for your birthday!" smiled Ma.

Going to the Staff-room, Anit complained to the class teacher –young and pretty Madam Paramjeet. And, all that she said was:

"Now, now, Anit, you know you have joined at mid-term. The others have been here longer. In fact, some of them have been here as long as we have, that is, since KG – the first class we opened this branch of the school with. They feel you are a newcomer, and they are only testing you."

"But ..."

"We took our admission test, isn't it?" said Madam Paramjeet. "Now they are taking theirs! Once you clear it, they will welcome you in as one of them!"

Anit walked away from the Staff-room. Suddenly, four boys from his class blocked his way. One of them shot out a kick, sending Anit sprawling, and smashing up a potted plant that was outside the Staff-room.

Just then, round the corridor there appeared the Principal Mr. Pradhan. Anit and his parents had heard that he had held the post even at the old location and for decades. Senior students too had had him as their Principal. Nobody could remember the school without "Stickler" in it.

An immaculately dressed man carrying a stout stick with a curved handle; Mr. Pradhan was very fond of the sentence "I am a stickler for discipline." That and possibly his stick had got him the nickname Stickler.

He had indeed looked intimidating at the admission interview. And now, it was most unnerving to look up at him from a sprawled position on the floor with all the pottery and plant scattered around him. The boys who had kicked him had vanished and Stickler held him responsible for the mess. He had to clear it up as a punishment.

The school-bus dropped him on the main road through the sector where Anit lived. From there, Anit had to walk a little to reach his block of flats with a guard at the gate. There stood several houses down the lane, all occupied except for one. It stood empty beyond a large but unkempt lawn. The others were smaller and hardly had any lawns. But they were peopled, mostly by young or middle-aged couples with school-going children. There was a small shop wedged in between them. Under a canopy, it sold fruits, vegetables, some groceries, biscuits, mineral water, and cold drinks. Bright streamers of shampoo and coffee sachets hung down from the canopy.

As he trudged along this road, Anit's heart swelled up within him, and he could not help saying out aloud:

"I wish I knew some magic to take care of those bullies."

A Stranger's Sympathy

"Is that so, kid?" A man at the shop abruptly turned around. He was in a blue robe that had silvery stars and half-moons worked out on it but was also full of patches. His toes stuck out of his shoes with curly tips. His skin was wrinkled and his hair grey. It stuck out from under an old, spangled turban with crushed plumes. He carried a tattered rucksack with one of its straps torn. He leant on a stick with, believe it or not, a star hanging down limply from its top.

Anit paused on his tracks.

The man turned back to the shopkeeper and said: "*Arrey yaar*, let me have a cold drink for free."

"No free business," said the shopkeeper.

"I am dying of thirst, but …"

He turned his coat pocket inside out and showed that it only had a hole in it. "Let me show you some magic, instead. Will that do for payment?"

"Magic! Are you a magician then?" The shopkeeper looked at the man and sniggered.

"Well, I do know a trick or two," said the man.

"I bet you do. You look every bit like a trickster. Now get lost."

Anit remembered that he still had some water left in his bottle.

Every day Ma made him take a bottle of mineral water to school. She did not trust the water at school to be germ-free.

Anit had been too upset today to open either his lunch-box or his bottle of water.

Now, he picked up the bottle and offered it to the man.

"You can have this," he said, "if you are so thirsty."

The man almost snatched it out of his hands and opened its cap. In one long draught, he finished all the water.

"Thanks, kid." He grinned at Anit.

"My lunch-box is there as well," said Anit. "You can have my lunch if you are hungry."

The man gave a twisted smile and gobbled up the *paneer tikkas* that Ma had given to Anit. He must have been hungry indeed.

"Now let me show you some magic even if you wouldn't give me a cold drink for it," the man called out to the shopkeeper. He puffed up his cheeks and blew at the canopy of the shop.

In a second, all the streamers of shampoo and coffee sachets got entangled with one another and tied themselves up into knots. The shopkeeper gave a yell and busied himself in sorting them out.

"Wow! That was magic!" Anit knew he should walk on, but he could not tear himself away from the spot. "How did you do it?"

"Before that, you tell me why you did not eat your lunch today? Good for me that you didn't, but why did you not have those great *paneer tikkas*? And why did you call out for some magic? Who are those bullies you want to give some magic treatment, eh?"

Anit had been told time and time again to be wary of strangers waylaying him. But, he was so upset today that he could not help opening up to the man. Anyway, his home was just in sight. There was nothing to get scared of. So, he did not run as the man began walking up with him. Instead, he told him all about how he was new to the area and being ragged at his new school. The man said nothing but "Hmmm" all the way. But his voice and eyes drew Anit out. Soon they had reached the gate to Anit's house. It was then that the man spoke out:

"Well, kid, I have the solution to your problems! Right in my rucksack!"

He brought out a velvet case from within and held it open.

His eyes popping out, Anit looked in.

Rings with sparkling stones, talismans with strange motifs, chains with talons as pendants!

"Are these magic?"

"*He He He He*," laughed the man.

"Well, you know, I *am* a magician. I do know magic. But my magic works only if the person, on whom I apply it, is the right one for it. My rings and talismans and chains do not always work. But if they get a chance with the right person, they are wonderful!"

Anit did not get it. The man started explaining again.

"See this ring," and he took out a silver one, studded with a red stone. "One who wears this can score runs as high as Virat Kohli – but only if the one is hundred per cent an honest man. Now, I have given it on trial to quite a few. But all of them have returned it – saying it doesn't work. Well, that doesn't mean that the ring is useless. It only means that the people who have tried it so far were not above a few lies. Anyway, it has not sold." The man gave out a sigh.

"Look at this chain. The claw on it is from – have a guess? Jatayu!"

Anit's jaw fell open. "Jatayu from the *Ramayana*?"

"None other," declared the man. "You know that as Ravana was kidnapping Sita, this old bird tried to stop him. He put up a great fight and then got killed. This is a claw that fell down during the fight, and a sage in the forest kept it with him. It was passed down through the ages – and came, well, to me."

"What can it do? This claw?"

"It can make someone fly – without an air-ticket, I mean!"

"But then why is it still with you? Why hasn't anyone bought it?"

The man grinned. "I did give it on a free trial to several. But the chain works only for someone who is really selfless and helpful to others – like Jatayu was. So far no one who has taken it has been up to that mark. And every time the chain has come back to me."

'Jatayu's claw!' Anit looked at the chain with awe.

"Go home, *beta*," the shopkeeper called out. "Don't stand there talking to *ajnavis*. It can be dangerous!"

"Absolutely right," said the man and waved at him. Immediately, the shopkeeper's cap flew off, and he had to run after it. He had to go after it again and again.

Meanwhile, the strange man turned to Anit, "Well, your mother will get worried if you waste time here with me and get late. But I have just the thing for you! It will protect you against any jabs and pokes your class-fellows may give you. Oh, it will do much more!"

"What is it?" Anit's eyes began to shine.

"It's a talisman–try it out!"

Anit found the man showing him a thin chain with a square locket imprinted with the image of Sun-god Surya.

"Free trial of seven days! *Aum Jabakusumasamkasham Kashyapeyam Mahadyutim !*" With that, the man quickly slipped the chain over Anit's head. It hung from his neck like a miniature of the breastplates that Anit had seen on the chests of the warriors in films and TV serials.

"I will come back after a week and take it back if it doesn't work," said the man.

He turned and trotted away, as Anit tucked the chain-and-locket inside his shirt and went home.

It was a Sunday the next day, and he would not have to go to school.

He examined the locket at leisure on Sunday. It was a tiny container really, with two parts that fitted together. On the lid, there was the carving of a smiling Sun.

"I wonder what is inside!" He prised it open and saw a scrap of something leathery, like shrivelled-up skin. Whatever it was, the metal against his skin gave him a tingling sensation, a mild charging of nerves. On his way from the school on Saturday, he had planned to ask his parents to complain to the Principal about his ragging. But now, he did not feel like cribbing. "I'll tackle it somehow on Monday," he said to himself.

Over the weekend, Ma caught sight of the chain as he was changing. She asked at once:

"What's that thing around your neck, Anit? I have never seen it before!"

"A boy in my class gave it to me," Anit fibbed.

"So you have started to make friends at school!" Ma did not say much more. She switched on the TV for the mythological serial, 'Karna'.

Next Week

"Attack!" As soon as he entered school on Monday, Anit saw his dreaded classmates lying in wait for him. He tried to walk past them. But a leg shot out and Anit fell flat on his knees on the pebbled pathway.

But, he was up the very next instant! The fall had not hurt him one bit. No bruises – in fact, no sense of impact.

It was as though there was something that came between his skin and the pebbles – a sheet of something – and took the blow.

Strange!

All through the Maths class, Sumant and Kireet threw paper aeroplanes at him. Actually, their tips can hurt quite a bit if they are made of stiff paper. Furthermore, it is tough to sit still in class with missiles hitting you from all sides.

Today, however, the missiles did not bother Anit at all. They reached him but it was as if they hit an invisible sheet covering Anit, and fell off.

Strange again!

The class got over, Anit picked up the paper missiles fallen around his feet and handed them over to Sumant politely.

"You have to try again," he said.

On Tuesday, the teasing began afresh.

Kireet jostled Anit as he was walking up to show his English Home Work. Anit hit his elbow at the edge of Kireet's bench. But he felt no sensation at all – as though between his elbow and the table there was a protective layer that had taken the entire impact. Kireet stared curiously as Anit continued to walk up to the teacher with an expressionless face.

At the PT period, the Physical Training instructor put Class Six on a game of racquet-ball.

"I want to play with Anit," said Sumant. Not at all happily, Anit faced Sumant.

Sumant hit hard and the balls like bullets tried to get Anit in his face and neck.

PT teacher shouted out a warning to Sumant, but he never listened.

Anit played defensive – fending off the balls as best as he could.

Khat! There came a ball finally that he could not tackle. It hit him right on his chest.

Anit fell back a little. He felt a little breathless. But that was all.

It was as if the ball had met something strong and stiff and flicked off against that resistance.

There was open astonishment on Sumant's face. The teacher who had rushed to catch Anit before he fell–as he should have done – stopped mid-way and stared.

Bimal, a student who had been standing there, watching the game, exclaimed:

"Wow, it's as though you are wearing invisible armour!"

'That is exactly how it feels,' Anit thought.

Next morning, as Anit was taking his bath before going to school, he took off his chain and placed it on the ledge of the bathroom window. While soaping himself, he slipped and fell. He knocked against the bath-tub, and felt pain shooting through his limbs.

He had had so many knocks in the past two days and was not hurt at all. Why was he hurt now?

As he dried himself and wore his chain again, Anit knew the

answer.

If AB leads to ab, and if AC leads to ac, then A is the cause of a. This is the Method of Agreement, as Anit had learnt at school.

If AB leads to ab, and if B leads to b, then too, A is the Cause of a. This is the Method of Difference.

When Anit wore the chain-and-locket, he felt no hurt or pain. When he took it off, he felt it again.

"I have found the magic that takes care of those bullies!"Anit shouted in the bathroom itself.

Wednesday was a repeat of Monday and Tuesday. Sumant and his group tried their usual tricks. Anit fell down, had paper missiles thrown at him, and so on. But he did not get hurt.

He smiled every time such an attempt was made. He began to quite enjoy himself.

Sumant scowled. Kireet snarled.

But what did Anit care?

In the evening, Anit sat doing his Home Work under Ma's watchful eyes.

Ma had her eye on the TV screen too; 'Karna' was going on.

Anit could not help catching bits of it.

Karna, the King of Anga, was standing ankle-deep in the flowing waters of the Ganga. He was praying to Surya, the Sun-god.

Aum Jabakusumasamkasham Kashyapeyam Mahadyutim.

'O Son of Sage Kashyapa, red as the Hibiscus, and shining with a great glow!'

The early morning sun was falling on his bowed head, as if in blessing.

Anit knew that Karna was really the son of Surya. His mother Kunti had prayed to Surya and received him as his blessing.

But as she had done so in secret, Kunti had thrown her baby into the river.

A charioteer from Hastinapur had found the baby floating

away in the water, and rescued it. The baby had been born with a thick layer of skin over his body and ears. Later, it had hardened to form a protective cover over him and he had come to be called *Saha-ja Kavacha-kundala* (One born with natural armour and ear-guards).Named Karna, he had grown up in Hastinapur as a warrior who considered himself better than Prince Arjuna, the younger brother of Prince Yudhishthira, heir-apparent to the throne of Hastinapur. But because he was thought to be a charioteer's son, he was denied a chance to test his skills against Arjuna in a public competition. So Prince Duryodhana, who contested Yudhishthira's claim, gave him the chance. He made Karna the king of Anga, a kingdom close to that of Hastinapur. Karna was ever so grateful to Duryodhana for this and vowed to be his friend all his life.

Prince Arjuna and his brothers – the five Pandavas – had Kunti as their mother. So Karna was really their brother. But nobody knew this, not even Karna. Karna saw himself as Duryodhana's friend. Duryodhana regarded the Pandavas as his enemies and tried in every way to stop them from having their place at the throne of Hastinapur.

In this, Karna was a big supporter of him.

Karna bathed every day in the river Ganga and prayed to the Sun-god.

Anyone who asked him for alms then, had his prayer fulfilled. Karna never refused anything that was asked of him at that hour.

On the TV screen, Karna was still praying when another figure came into the TV screen. Arjuna's patron-god Indra, disguised as a poor man asking for alms.

"Pray, give me your natural armour and ear-guards!"

"But I was born with them!"protested Karna. "They are a part of my body. My natural protection from enemies! Take anything else you want."

The serial ended there and Ma, having no interest in the next serial, switched the TV off.

Anit sat there, with Home Work forgotten.

He felt he had just realized what the leathery piece in his talisman was.

On Thursday, when Anit got on to the school-bus, he did so like a warrior mounting a chariot.

The timid steps of a newcomer were gone.

In the class, Madam Paramjeet was calling up students for board work.

Sumant sent a paper missile at the back of Anit's neck. Anit turned back, and said, “Look, enough is enough. Stop your guerrilla warfare and let's have an open fight.”

“Oh yeah?” hissed Sumant. “You think you can take me on?”

“I can,” Anit's voice rang out bold and clear.

“Okay, Anit,” called Madam Paramjeet from the other end of the classroom. “Come up to the board. I am so glad you volunteered.”

In the lunch-break, Kireet and Sumant came up to Anit.

“So, you want an open fight, do you?”

“Yes, I do,” said Anit. “I am tired of your bully tactics. I am new to this school, alright. But you can't go on ragging me forever.”

“No? How are you going to stop us?” said Kireet.

Bimal came forward. “Let there be a showdown as Anit said. If Anit can hold on his own against Sumant, we'll take him as one of us. Sumant and Kireet must stop pestering him.”“And if he can't?” sneered Kireet, “We can then have some more fun with him, can't we?”

“No chance of that!” said Anit, his head held high.

On Friday at lunch-break, at a quiet corner of the playground, Anit and Sumant faced each other – as in a wrestling arena. Others stood in a ring around them. Someone whistled, and the match began.

Sumant dealt the first blow. He balled his fist and hit hard but Anit just felt a small push. It was Sumant who jumped back as though his knuckles were smarting.

Anit now dealt him a blow that had him doubled up in pain.

He was feeling a great strength surge through him. He could feel the talisman against his chest, and it set his body a-tingle. Sumant hit again, but it felt like feather-touch. Anit hit back. As the match went on, sweat broke out on Sumant's body. The sun was in mid-sky and beat down upon the two with an angry force.

But Anit felt neither the hurt nor the heat, as he fought on with the fellow who had bullied him all these weeks.

Sumant was clearly getting tired. His knees were buckling.

Anit stood his ground. Sumant took something out of his pocket and hit Anit right on the chest with concentrated fury. Anit did feel a sharp impact but grabbed Sumant's fist and wrenched that something out .Why, it was a divider out of the geometry box !He quickly stuffed it into his pocket and charged Sumant head-on. Sumant lost his balance and fell down– at an 'awkward angle'.

"Come on! Get up!" shouted the students who had gathered round them. "One, Two, Three…"But Sumant did not seem to be able to get up. Had he fainted away?

Bimal rushed to get their class teacher. Kireet ran for water to splash on Sumant. Another boy went for the First Aid Box. Others bent over Sumant.

Yet others thronged round Anit.

"You are a champion!"

"Sumant could do nothing to you!"

"You are great, Anit!"

"Sumant is nothing to you!"

"He used underhand means! This was a boxing match!"

"The divider could have hurt you badly."

"Divider?" Anit raised his eyebrows. "I never saw any divider."

He knew Sumant would get into deep trouble if he reported the matter of the divider to the school authorities. But now that he had won over him, Anit did not feel like harassing him.

“What do you mean?” said the others. “We all saw him hit you with it. It fell down somewhere.”

They looked for it but could not find it. So Sumant was spared a very big charge. Some of the boys did indeed mention the divider to the P.T. teacher. But Anit himself denied seeing or feeling any divider being thrust at him. The divider sat safely in the pocket of his shorts. Sumant sat safely in the sick-room. The matter never reached Stickler.

When school was over, and Anit was boarding the school-bus, Kireet and a few others of their group came over. Sumant too was with them, though he looked pale.

“You win, Anit,” Kireet grinned. “Ragging is over for you.”

“I’ll never pester you again.” Sumant’s voice was trembling, “You are now one of us. And thanks for being quiet about the —”

“Oh, that’s alright,” Anit said warmly.

“But tell me something. How come you didn’t get hurt by it? How come you didn’t seem to mind any of the blows I gave you? Not just today but for the last couple of days?” Sumant looked puzzled.

“How come things seem to simply bounce back from you?” echoed Kireet. “Is it magic?”

That evening, there was ‘Karna’ again.

Anit too watched it with Ma.

“I want no other alms but your natural armour and ear-guards,” Indra was saying to Karna.

“But,” Karna tried to reason, “that means cutting them off from my body.”

“What about your vow that you never refuse any alms?”

“Ask some other alms of me. Wealth, land, gems – anything! Let my *kavacha-kundala* be. If I slice them off, I’ll have no defence against arrows and spears and swords –no defence against Arjuna.”

But Indra was unrelenting, “Aren’t you known as Data-Karna? Karna, the Generous? Is it for nothing?”

The next scene had Karna slicing off leathery layers from his body. Some bits fell down on the ground like wood shavings. At one stage, even the portions around the ears were sliced off. Karna gave them all away to Indra and the episode ended for the day.

Anit clutched at Ma.

"Ma, I have got a bit of that armour with me. They must have fallen on the ground, and Indra didn't take them. It is one of those pieces that are there in the talisman..."

"What are you talking about?" Ma looked as though Anit was out of his senses.

Bit by bit, the story came out.

Baba laughed his head off when he heard it.

"Karna's *kavacha*! I have never heard a better one!"

"Confidence-trickster- that's what he was!" said Ma. "And hadn't I told you never to talk to strangers?"

They made Anit take off the talisman and show it to them.

Baba opened it up and peered at the leathery scrap inside.

"Well, it does seem like a dried bit of skin," he said, "but wait!"

He felt it gingerly and roared, "Why it's plastic – torn from some stupid shopping bag!"

Ma too examined it. "Anit, you have been an idiot!"

"But it did things for me!" cried Anit. "It saved me all the week from all Sumant's blows and Kireet's pokes."

"That was only your feeling, Anit," Ma put her arms round Anit. "You thought you had a talisman. So you felt protected."

"How much did that man sell this to you for?" asked Baba.

"I told you, he gave it to me on a free trial. He said he'll come in seven days to find out if it had worked."

"That's tomorrow, isn't it? You said he gave it to you last Saturday?" said Baba. "Well, I'll talk to the watchman of the Residents' Welfare Association. If he does come over to the block, he'll turn him over to the police."

"No, Baba, please don't," Anit got into a panic. "He's a poor fellow, Baba, didn't even have money for a cold drink. Don't hand him over to the police!"

"At any rate, you are not to wear that silly thing again!" said Ma.

Anit did not wear the talisman round his neck any more but took it with him in his pocket as he went to school the next day.

"What if those bullies try to hurt me today? What if Sumant and Kireet do not keep their word?" He was worried all his way on the bus.

But there was no need to be worried.

As Anit entered school, there were friendly 'Hi's and 'Hello's. Sumant and Kireet, who were also entering, gave him a mock salute. In the class, Anit saw a new respect for him in the eyes of his class-fellows. Nobody jostled him or poked him in the ribs with rulers. No paper missiles came and hit him. No legs shot out at him to trip him down. At lunch, Mayank offered him *samosa*s from his lunch-box. Sumant surprised him by holding out a palm-full of jujubes.

Even a couple of seniors, like Head-boy Sanjay and Head-girl Tarini, said 'Hello' to him of their own accord. So did Ranjit, who had the general reputation of being a senior with some mischief in him.

They must have heard reports of the incident.

But Anit could not be entirely happy. Half his mind was wondering if the man would be there today to find out whether his talisman had worked. The 'free trial' of seven days would be over this afternoon.

As he got down from the bus on the main road, Anit saw that the man was there, at the cold drinks' shop down the lane that led to his block.

Anit ran to him. "It worked! They've stopped ragging me!"

The man's face lit up. "I knew it would work! That's why I gave it to you!"

"And I know what it is!" said Anit. "It's a piece of Karna's *kavacha*. Isn't it?"

"*He He He He,*" laughed the man. "I knew you would figure that out! I also knew it would work for you though it had never worked with anyone else before!"

"What made you feel it would work with me?"

"Because you gave me a drink from your bottle. And your lunch – water to the thirsty and food to the hungry! I knew you to be generous of heart, someone for whom the *kavacha* of Karna the Generous would work. And I was right!"

"What will you sell the magic talisman for?" asked Anit. "Now that the 'free trial' is over? I took out money from my piggy-bank today."

"Oh well, let me see," the man said with a wink. "What about buying me a cold drink?"As they sipped cold drinks together, Anit blurted out, "Baba was saying it was just a bit of plastic!"

"He could be right, kid."

"But – but – it works! It's magic."

"It is not the material that makes it something magical. It is the secret chant that makes it so. In the East, it is *mantrashakti*, and in the West it is *abracadabra*. It charges the most familiar or mundane object with magic. *He He He He*."

His voice grew serious.

"Keep it if it works for you! If it's magic for you!"

Then he turned round the corner and vanished.

A New Chore

In a couple of weeks, Anit settled down in the new neighbourhood. He found that four of his schoolmates lived nearby and now they were quite happy to take them into their circle. They were Bimal, Chandan and pig-tailed Deeksha who was just as good as them at cricket. He began to hang around with them.

This Sunday, they had decided to have a cricket-match among themselves in the nearby park, and Anit was hurrying to it.

The house that had been empty for so long had very recently been taken by an elderly couple, the Naths. Anit knew that for quite a few months now, Bimal, Chandan, and Deeksha had considered the house and its grounds as their own property. They had used the shed at the back for playing hide-and-seek, and its unkempt lawns for playing cricket, football or tennis. An impressive-looking lock hung on the front gate, but it was easy to swing over the low garden wall. And though the wooden front door with its 'Yale' lock was an insurmountable barrier, they had discovered how to enter through the bathroom at the back, whose huge window had lost its glass pane. They had free access to the empty interiors of the house, complete rights of egress and ingress.

But with the coming of the Naths, they had been shooed out unceremoniously. In fact, Mr. Nath had visited all their parents with lists of damages that he thought (rightly) the children had done to the house. The parents had refused to pay up for past offences, which in any case could not be proved. But they had assured Mr.Nath, there would be no further damages on account of their children. They would see to that, they had promised Mr.Nath, looking darkly at their children. Not perfectly satisfied, Mr. Nath had taken to muttering and sputtering as the children went past their house to school, to the nearby park, or to the local store. Bimal, Chandan and Deeksha had thus developed a tendency to go past their house quicker than they did those of others. It had rubbed off on Anit as well and he too quickened his steps as he walked past the Nath residence.

But a voice called out to him, "You child!"

It was Mr. Nath. Waving a newspaper, and beckoning to him.

"What now?" wondered Anit, as he stopped in his tracks.

"Come closer," growled Mr. Nath, and so Anit had to.

"Can you read out this paper to me?" asked Mr Nath.

Anit's jaws fell open in dismay. What about the cricket match he was going off to play with his friends at the park? Glorious sunshine bathed the world in Sunday spirits and the air was crisp and fresh. To read out the paper to Mr. Nath seemed nothing short of punishment.

"W-what have I done?"

"Done? Well, nothing," said Mr. Nath, sounding a little surprised. "It's just that these days I'm having some difficulty reading the small print, and you can help me out instead of being a general nuisance like the other children around here. As a favour."

Anit remembered that Karna never refused any favour that was asked of him.

With a small sigh, he went up to Mr. Nath. While Mr. Nath lay in an easy chair, Anit sat on a cane stool next to him, and read out the headlines. Tax Commission Submits Interim Report, Hottest Day in 20 Years, Elderly Couple Murdered, Stolen Antiques Recovered, Shooting at the Border, and so on.

He then had to read out the columns under whichever headline caught Mr. Nath's fancy.

Nearby, a youngish fellow in shorts watered the plants. Anit observed that the weeds had been cleared in the garden and new plants planted. Flowerbeds had been marked out in bricks.

The young fellow was watering them with a hosepipe fitted to a tap beside the gate. Water fell in shining arcs upon the earth, bringing out its fresh green smell.

The sun grew strong. Anit's throat got dry, but Mr. Nath did not ask him to stop. He lay back on the easy chair, utterly relaxed, eyes closed, waggling a slipper dangling on one leg crossed upon the other.

Suddenly there were hoots of laughter. Anit looked up and caught sight of Bimal, Chandan and Deeksha, his friends, standing beyond the gate, laughing obviously at his predicament. They must have wondered why he was late and had come back to look for him.

Their laughter jerked Mr.Nath out of his happy mood. "You again!" He shouted at Bimal, Chandan, and Deeksha. "Oh, alright. You are 'off' now," he said more kindly to Anit. "Go and join your friends! But don't let them take you over completely! Come next Sunday as well. I know you have school on other days."

Anit was only too glad to get up and go. "Wait a bit," said Mr. Nath. "Gaju! Get some *laddus* from Amma," he ordered the fellow watering the plants. Gaju threw away the hose carelessly and went in. In a moment, he was back with a couple of *laddus* and a glass of water. Saying his 'Thanks' quickly, Anit downed a *laddu* with some water and made off, almost tripping over the hose, which lay there, spewing water and making a small puddle.

He ran and caught up with Bimal, Chandan and Deeksha. It was near eleven now, but he could still have a go at the game.

"Why did you waste half the whole morning?" asked Deeksha angrily. So far as cricket was concerned, she was every bit as enthusiastic as any of them.

As Anit explained, Bimal exclaimed impatiently, "Why can't he just hear the news on TV!"

"Why can't he have his eyes treated, instead of making you read for him!" grumbled Chandan.

Dadi Arrives

It was evening and Anit was busy doing his Home Work when Ma announced that Dadi was arriving that day. Baba had received her telegram at the office and gone straight to the railway station to receive her. Dadi was Baba's favourite aunt, the widow of a brother of Anit's grandfather. She lived with her son, Uncle Samit, in Patna but came at least once a year to visit them. "Be on your best behaviour before her," Ma said. "Don't let her say '*Bahu*, you are not bringing up your child properly.'"

In an hour, Dadi arrived.

She had a face like a ripe, red mango, Anit often thought. She was always dressed in glistening white, and everything looked dusty and grey beside her.

"Where's Annu? Where's the little one?" Anit could hear her cry as she got down from the car.

Anit did not care much for that name but he went down at once.

"Here's the little one!" Dadi hugged Anit tight. She smelt as always, of betel-leaves and cardamom, ever since Anit could remember.

The next moment, the usual comments began.

"Oh, how thin and dark he's become! *Bahu*, he's just skin and bones!"

"I've grown taller, Dadi, that is why I'm looking thinner."

"Oh. What nonsense, it's just that you have not been drinking your milk. *Bahu*, didn't I tell you the last time that you must give him a glass of milk every day?"

"Ma does give it to me, Dadi, but I pour it back into the pan most of the days. I hate milk."

"Oh my God, I have never heard of such a thing. *Bahu*, you must keep a closer watch over him."

And so it went on.

Dadi brought lots of gifts every time she came. Home-made jams and pickles, and such sweetmeat as no *mithai* shop held. *Saris* for Ma, *dhotis* for Baba, and *pajamas* for Anit. Last time, Anit had told her to cut out the *pajamas*.

"What I like are jeans and Bermudas," he had told her.

She had given him a lecture in return.

"When we were your age, we had decided to wear only what is Indian. *Swadeshi*. You see, Gandhiji had called out to all of us. It's a sad thing that your generation has no one like him to call out to you."

She had made Anit go out to play in *pajama-kurta*, and got very cross when Anit had returned with the *pajamas* torn at the knee and the *kurta* at the armpit.

But had that stopped her from bringing a fresh load of *pajama-kurtas* for Anit this time? No. There they were in a stiff pile.

Anit knew it was not much use protesting. He had to wear them, at least while Dadi was around.

Dadi also disapproved of his playing video-games on Baba's iPad.

"At his age, he should not be sitting hunched up before machines. It'll ruin his eyes. *Bahu*, don't let him. Annu, my little one, it's outdoor sports that build the body up."

She also disliked cards. Anit wanted to show her a simple magic trick with cards that he had picked up at school. "None of that, little Annu. I can't stand card games – or magic."

Anit wanted to tell her about his magic talisman but thought better of it.

Stickler Is Going

Bimal, Chandan and Deeksha lived nearby and went to the same school as Anit, and so they met every morning at the bus stop. A few days after Dadi's arrival, on Saturday to be exact, they were planning their Sunday.

"We'll hold a one-day match," suggested Chandan.

They had an ongoing rivalry with some other kids in the neighbourhood and they busied themselves in preparing a match with them. Then the bus came with its load of other children from other localities.

School that day was different. News came that Stickler was leaving!

"You see, he's 60 and that's the retirement age," Madam Paramjeet explained as she announced the news to her class. "There are rules for how long one can go on working. If you are too young, you cannot, and if you are too old, you can't either. For most jobs, if you are under 21, you are too young to work. If you are above 60, you are too old."

"But St – Principal Sir – isn't too old!" exclaimed Anit.

"If he is above 60, he is," said Madam Paramjeet. "And he's going to be sixty in a couple of weeks."

Stickler – who strode around the whole school waving his stick like some knight with his lance – too old for work? Stickler – who stood so upright at the Assembly every morning – too old? Stickler – who could make the boldest of boys crumple up – too old?

Anit wondered.

Soon senior boys from Classes 11 and 12 began to go to other classes with requests for contributions.

"We have to present him a grand token of our appreciation for his services," said Sanjay, the Head-boy.

"We're planning to present him a silver replica of the school building," supplemented Tarini, the Head-girl.

But even they could not hide the cheerfulness in their voices.

Stickler had been so generally unpopular! His going was good news.

"Thank God, Stickler's going," Most of the students whispered to one another. "He's made life here worse than in an army."

Ranjit of Class 11 had gone even further. Anit had been sent out to fetch some chalk for his own class from the Staff-room, and overheard Ranjit tell a few senior students that he would be celebrating that evening.

"How that Stickler pulled me down before the entire school last year! He announced right in the Assembly that I had been caught copying in the Pre-test! I'll never forgive him for that."

"You *had* copied, you know," said Tarini.

"But there was no need to announce it in the Assembly. I had pleaded with him not to do so; even my father. But no, all he would say was: I am a stickler for discipline! Well, I'm not one bit sorry that he's on his way out."

"Does that mean," Sanjay asked, "that you won't help us in arranging his Farewell?"

"Well. I certainly won't go out of my way to – no, wait a bit," replied Ranjit. "Actually, I'm so glad he's going that I'll do all I can to make his Farewell a grand success. You can count on me, Sanjay; I'll do any amount of running around for you."

"Good," said Sanjay briefly. "Now listen, all of you –" And he went on to assign duties and plan details.

Anit hurried back to his class with the chalk. He knew he had taken more time than he should have and was in for a firing. That made him run so fast that he collided with someone as he turned the corner.

Someone erect and immaculate, carrying a stick with a curved handle.

"I don't allow my boys to run amok like this, don't you know?" said the Principal in a chilling voice.

"Sorry, Sir," came Anit's automatic reply.

"That's not good enough. You will stand here facing the wall for the rest of the hour."

"But Ma'am sent me out for some chalk, Sir, she'll be waiting."

"Fine, go and give her the chalk and come back here."

Red in the face, Anit walked up to his class, handed over the chalk, explained everything to his teacher, and went out again.

"Don't go back," called out someone from his class. "He didn't ask your name or class. How is he going to catch you out?"

Anit shook his head. He knew Stickler would be waiting for him. He was such a stickler.

An Important Match

'The match, it's today!'

The thought burst across Anit's brain as soon as he opened his eyes the next morning.

Baba slept late every Sunday, but this Sunday he was up early. That was on account of Dadi who was a firm believer in getting up early. It was a tenet with her. She would be up even as the day broke, and, facing the east, begin chanting her hymn to the Sun-god.

Jabakusumasamkasham kashyapeyam mahadyutim

Dhvantarim sarvapapaghnam pranatosmi divakaram.

"O brilliant son of sage Kashyapa,

The one who creates the day and removes all sin

The one who is like the red Hibiscus!

I bow to you!"

Then she would go up to each of them and urge them to get up. "How can you miss out on this absolutely splendid morning!" she would scold.

"Look out of your window. See the pink in the sky. Hear those birds. Breathe in that fresh air. And then tell me if you still want to go back to your sleep."

Neither Baba nor Ma ever said, 'Yes' to that question. That

made it even more difficult for Anit to do so. In fact, he had realized from her earlier visits that as long as Dadi was around, it was best to do as she said, and get up early. Besides, wasn't this the prayer the roadside magician had chanted when he gave Anit his talisman?

And this Sunday morning, it did feel good to be up and about early, with the day waiting for him to come and take it up in his hands. He felt sure that he would play superbly today, and so would the rest of the team.

For breakfast, there was puffed rice in milk. After Dadi's arrival, bread, cheese-spread or cornflakes had been discarded (temporarily, Anit knew). Instead, there was *muri* (puffed rice) with bananas, in bowls of sweetened milk. Well, it did taste good and was filling as well.

Chandan had proper cricket bats and would bring them along. Bimal, who was a good fast-bowler, would bring the balls. Deeksha would bring the wickets. Though not in very great condition, they would serve their purpose. The other team would, of course, bring its own bats.

Bidding everyone a cheerful 'Bye', Anit sauntered forth.

He went past the houses along the lane, whistling to himself, thinking only of the great day ahead.

The vegetable-vendor – a sixty-year-old named Padam – was vending vegetables. His wooden cart was laden with fresh vegetables. He was shouting his familiar cry of "*Sabzi lo! Taza sabzi!*" and people were coming up to his cart, feeling and testing the vegetables with their hands. Loading them into plastic bowls kept on the cart, passing the bowls to Padam to be weighed. Bargaining, haggling.

Padam had grey in his hair, but his cry was loud and robust. Every day he made his rounds, pushing the cart by his handles, parking it at certain steady customers' houses, and then moving on again.

Pappu, his puppy, tied with a rope to the handle of the cart, moved on with Padam.

"Fresh vegetables! The freshest of them!" cried Padam.

As it was Sunday, there were no children in uniforms with shoulders sagging under the weight of their schoolbags, no office-goers with briefcases. There were fewer vehicles, and fewer people. Even the sun seemed to climb up the sky a little slower than usual.

Who would win the toss today? Their team or the other? How would the match go? Would they be able to thrash their opponents? Would he be able to hit sixes?

Suddenly, there was a cry of "You child!"

Lost in thoughts of the match, Anit had not realized that he had come up to the redbrick house of the Naths. He had not hastened his steps and in any case, that would not have helped. For, Mr. Nath stood right at the gate, looking his way.

At the sight of the newspaper in his hand, Anit realized that he had clean forgotten all about reading the paper out to Mr. Nath.

Well, Mr. Nath certainly hadn't.

For a second, Anit thought that he would simply run for it.

Old Mr. Nath could not catch him, could he?

But something within him said, "Look Anit, you can't, you had agreed to read to him today, at least you hadn't had the guts to say `no', and that was before you had planned the match. You have to read to him, at least a little before you go to play your match."

So this Sunday as well, Anit settled down on a cane stool beside Mr. Nath on his easy chair, while Gaju watered the plants with his hose.

"No Consensus on Election Dates – Brutal Murder of 75-Year-Old – Plane Crashes over the Indian Ocean," he started to read out.

He had not proceeded much when a thin cry came floating out from inside the house.

"Gaju-u-u- are you dead or what? Can't you hear me calling?"

As a matter of fact, no calls for Gaju had reached there. But Mr. Nath began to shout at Gaju. "Hear that? Amma is crying herself hoarse for you, and here you are – not paying any heed."

Gaju did not reply back, but quietly put down the hose and went in.

Anit read on, but Mr. Nath seemed not to pay close attention. After a while, he gestured Anit to stop and said, more to himself than to Anit: "She's so helpless –"

Anit had never thought that Mr. Nath could speak in such a soft tone.

Gaju came out and began to water the plants once again.

After a few minutes of fidgeting, Mr. Nath suddenly said, "Let's go in and look her up."

He put a hand on Anit's shoulder and Anit found himself going in with him. Bimal, Chandan and Deeksha had told him that the house was all dusty and deserted. But now the walls were freshly painted in pink; the windows had maroon curtains and the floors shone. There were lots of highly-polished wooden furniture, and books in rich bindings. But what struck Anit was that scattered here, there, and everywhere, were broken bits of statues, carvings and pottery.

"Antique pieces, all of them," remarked Mr. Nath, following Anit's gaze.

He then went into a heavily curtained room where a frail old lady lay on a bed. Exquisitely pretty in a lacy gown, with silver hair falling over her thin shoulders, and resting on huge pillows. Anit stared. Could anyone look so delicate, so fragile?

But the next moment, the spell was broken.

"That Gaju, he's useless," the lady spoke out in a harsh, complaining tone. "And who's this brat?"

"The one who read out the paper to me last week. Remember I asked for some *laddus* for him? I called him here today as well." There was a chair beside the bed, next to a bookshelf full of books as well as knick-knacks. And with a stone Buddha on top. Mr. Nath sat down on the chair. "But, tell me what Gaju's done?"

The lady immediately plunged into an account of Gaju's wrong-doings. He had forgotten that he had to add sugar to the health drink the lady took, he had not given it in her favourite cup, and he had not been at hand when she had finished it and wanted the empty cup to be taken away.

"For that matter, where were *you* when I was calling for Gaju? Outside, with that newspaper. You're never beside me when I want you."

The old lady's voice had such bitterness that Anit looked at her once more. What was her problem? Why was she so querulous? Why was she in bed on such a glorious morning?

"Go away now and leave me in peace," said the lady, most unfairly, thought Anit.

"Yes, yes," said Mr. Nath, "Come, child, let us go back to our newspaper."

For a second, he looked like a schoolboy who had been scolded. And that enabled Anit to come out with what he had been longing to say all this time, "I have to go now. I have a match to play."

"A match?" Mr. Nath stopped halfway to the front door.

"A cricket match – Block A versus Block B," Anit informed him.

"I see," said Mr. Nath, beginning to move towards the door once more. "So all this while, I've been keeping you away from your match."

Anit nodded yes as he came out of the house, Mr. Nath by his side. Sure enough, Bimal, Chandan and Deeksha were hanging around outside the gate. They gestured impatiently at Anit.

Mr. Nath saw them but made no signs of leaving Anit's side.

They reached the gate together, and then he turned to Anit and asked: "Where do you people hold your match? I'll come and watch."

"Anything as long as you let me go," muttered Anit under his breath.

What he said aloud was: "Of course."

Mr. Nath shouted out to Gaju that he was going out for a short while. "Tell *Amma* and stay near her."

To Anit and the others, he said, "Cricket is a game I adore. Do you know I even took a test in umpiring and qualified? In my days, I have umpired important Inter-State matches. Well, don't you need an umpire for this important match of yours?"

By the end of the match, Mr. Nath had become a friend to them.

Dadi Has A Secret

As the days passed, Anit sensed that Dadi had a secret. She was somehow different this time. As jolly as ever, as forceful, she was nevertheless not quite the same as on her former visits. She had brought a huge leather bag with her and she kept on peering into it from time to time. No one had any idea what it contained and Dadi always kept it within easy reach. Then again, Anit sometimes caught her working out some numbers on slips of paper, then tearing them up, and working them out again and again. Sometimes she lost the thread of the conversation and sunk into her own thoughts. What was more, she was quite angry when Anit pointed out this to her.

She had also come unexpectedly this time. Usually, she came in February when Delhi was at its most pleasant. But now it was October.

That apart, more than once she had gone out all by herself, and as a rule, she never did that. "Delhi is such a terrible place," she usually grumbled, "I can never find my way about in it." She insisted on Ma accompanying her while shopping, or Baba dropping her to her friends' houses. But this time, even though it was Gurgaon she had come to, and not Delhi, she ventured out alone in taxis.

"But *Chachi*," Baba had said in surprise the first time she declared such an intention, "You'll get lost."

That made Dadi flare up. "Ravi, I'm not so stupid as that!"

"But you have always said that you would get lost if you go out alone in Delhi," retorted a bewildered Baba.

"Don't argue with me, Ravi, my child. You know I don't like it."

"Yes, but –" said Baba and gave up. Even Baba did not dare argue with Dadi.

Anit was actually quite fond of Dadi, especially because she never forgot to bring jams and pickles especially for him. She remembered that Anit preferred pickled tamarind, and was mad about orange marmalade. Over the years, on her visits, she had seen Anit grow up and Anit too was comfortably familiar with her ways.

So when he noticed Dadi's solitary sprees, he was perplexed. He shared his perplexity with his friends one evening in the park, after their games.

"Do you think she's going to some doctor in secret?" asked Deeksha, thoughtfully fingering her plaits.

"Why should she do that?" said Anit. "She always wants us to come along when she goes to see doctors. Last time she had to have all her teeth out and she made Ma sit beside her through every single session."

"What if your Dadi feels she has got cancer or AIDS?" said Bimal. "Something that's incurable, something that people dread? She might not then like to take anyone along with her when she goes to the doctor."

"Yeah, some people like to face that sort of thing alone," added Deeksha slowly. "My grandfather – he's dead now – had kept it hidden from us that he had cancer. We came to know of it only in the last stages. He used to live all by himself in our country home and his letters were always so cheerful that we never suspected that there was anything wrong with him."

Anit felt fear clutching at his heart.

Dadi was quite terrible at times – but he did not want her to die. Oh no. He wanted her to be less of a tyrant, but he did want her to live.

Meanwhile, Bimal was going on: "We must find out where she goes."

"Yes, we must," echoed Deeksha.

"Anit," ordered Chandan, "the next time she says she's going out alone, tell us at once. We'll follow her."

"Yes, that's right," agreed Anit.

Together, they made up their mind that Dadi's secret must come out.

"But what if she *does* have cancer?" asked Bimal. "What are we going to do then?"

"Well, we must tell Baba and Ma about it and make them take her to the best doctors – not just this one doctor she's seeing in secret."

"And also, we must be very nice to her," added Chandan. "Do exactly as she says, be helpful to her and so on."

"Yes, we must all be very nice to her," repeated Deeksha.

It so happened that just then Dadi made her appearance round the corner. She had accompanied Ma to the nearby mall Hong Kong Bazaar, and her hands, like Ma's, were laden with shopping bags. Deeksha was the first to run up to her and offer to carry them for her.

"That's a good girl," said Dadi and relieved herself of a couple of bags.

Then Chandan went up to her with the same offer, followed by Bimal.

A little surprised, Dadi nevertheless gave them a packet each to carry.

So by the time Anit went up to her, she had just one bag with her and she waved Anit off.

"I'm quite capable of carrying this myself – my bones still have strength in them," she said. 'Did she put a little too much stress on the word 'still'?' Anit wondered.

Planning the Farewell

"I won't hear of the school giving me a farewell," Anit heard Stickler declare in the assembly. Every morning at 8.30, the students assembled in the school grounds. So did the staff, headed by the Principal.

The trees along the compound walls waved their heads in greeting as the sun sent down its rays to strike the huge brass gong on the dais where the staff stood. Anit loved this moment. It set the tone of the whole day for him.

While Stickler talked on about the various ideals his students should have, the various pitfalls they should guard against, Anit would look at the sunny skies and the waving trees. When the band played and the school song was sung, only then did he join in (untunefully).

But today he was struck by Stickler's words.

"The correct thing is that the person who's leaving must bid the farewell. Haven't you heard of the book *A Farewell to Arms*? It's the man there who is bidding farewell to weapons, that is, moving away from warfare. The arms are not bidding farewell to the man, are they? So why should you, whom I'm leaving behind, hold a farewell function for me? It should be the other way around."

"But all around us, we see just the opposite, Sir." Sanjay the Head-boy was bold enough to interrupt.

"I know. I know. You see the school giving a farewell to Class

12, which is going to take the Board Exams. You see the college giving a farewell to the outgoing Third Year. You hear of people giving farewell to the colleague who is leaving or the boss who is retiring. Yes. But that does not make it right, does it? No, I will not allow such a wrong thing to be done in my case. I'm a stickler for details, and you all know that."

It was a dampener. Anit knew that everyone had looked forward to the Farewell – not because they were overly fond of Stickler, but because it promised some zestful variety in the everyday school-life.

Curiously enough, he found Ranjit minding even more than the rest.

During recess that day, in the course of a game of hide-and-seek, Anit was hiding from his pursuer behind a pile of bricks. The Gymnasium was being built and bricks lay piled all around.

As he crouched there, Anit realized that Sanjay and Ranjit were on the other side of the pile.

There was a big *jamun* tree overlooking the pile of bricks and the two senior boys were probably just resting under its shade.

"But Sanjay, can't you do something about his going away?"

"Ranjit, *yaar*, what can I do? Stickler's said that he doesn't want a farewell."

"But we can't let him go without showing him our gratitude for all he's done to us, I mean, for us. We'll feel horrid. No, Sanjay, you are the Head-boy. You should do something about it."

"Dash it, Ranjit, I know I should. But what?"

"Well, we can still present him that silver replica of the school building. It needn't be a big ceremony. We can just go up to him in the Assembly and present it to him on the day he's going."

"Yes." Sanjay's tone brightened. "Let's do that at least."

Just then there was a cry of "Got you!" and Anit's pursuer descended upon him.

Anit could hear no more.

But he agreed wholeheartedly with whatever Ranjit had said.

He lost no time in telling his classmates what he had overheard. They all felt that Stickler just had to be given a farewell – all the more because he did not want one. Later in the day, Sanjay and Ranjit and a few other senior students began their rounds of the classes, asking for contributions. This time there was a hush-hush secrecy about the way in which they did it. If Stickler knew what they were doing, he would clearly put a stop to it. Every class promised to do its bit, with the same air of secrecy.

A silver replica of the school building, yes, that was the right memento, felt everybody. The seniors collected photographs of the school from the office, saying that they wanted it for the school magazine that they edited (largely) by themselves. Ranjit said that his parents knew a clever silversmith, and he was assigned the job of getting the replica made.

Trailing Dadi

It was a Saturday evening.

"No, you needn't come with me, *Bahu*," said Dadi to Ma. "I'll be fine on my own."

"You are not so familiar with Gurgaon, *Chachi*," protested Ma. "Let me come along."

"Don't bother, *Bahu*."

"But it's not a bother, *Chachi*. I'm quite free today."

"If you're free, *Bahu*, clean out your kitchen cupboards. It must have been ages since you did that."

As soon as this conversation had started, Anit had moved over to the landline telephone. What a pity, he thought, that he did not yet have a cell phone of his own.

After a hurried phone conversation with Bimal, he told Ma that he was going over to Chandan's.

An hour later, Dadi (and Dadi alone) started out in the local taxi that had been called for her. With her, she had her big leather bag. Anit, along with Bimal, Chandan and Deeksha, followed her in another from the same local taxi service.

The taxi sped through the busy traffic, passing Chhatarpur and Qutab Minar. Why, it was going to Delhi!

Bimal looked questioningly at the taxi driver. Not all taxis plied between Delhi and Gurgaon, which however close to Delhi, was altogether in a different State, Haryana.

But the taxi driver nodded reassuringly to him and carried on. Passing Hauz Khas, and Yusuf Sarai, it took a turn towards

Green Park. "Uncle, don't let that taxi out of sight," pleaded Chandan.

"Uncle, faster," urged Deeksha.

"*Bachhon* (children), I don't like this at all," said the driver of the taxi. He lived in a lane off the street where Deeksha lived, and knew all of them by sight. In fact, when they had been younger, he had, on a monthly agreement, taken Bimal, Chandan and Deeksha to their play-school.

."Uncle, it's alright," Chandan assured him, as the four of them sitting close together, followed the taxi in front. The taxi drew to a stop in a small and crowded place called Arjun Nagar near Safdarjung Enclave. Dadi got down and asked the taxi to wait. She then went into an alley of Arjun Nagar.

Asking their taxi to park a little away from Dadi's, Anit and the others followed, of course, at a distance from Dadi.

The narrow alley led through small barber-shops, tailoring shops, stationery shops, Photostat centres and buildings with 'To Let' signs.

Almost at its very end, there was a building – an old building that had been extended and expanded haphazardly over the years. At the narrow entrance there hung a shabby board, saying 'The Lodge'.

Dadi went in.

"This can't be a clinic or nursing home!" exclaimed Anit.

It certainly could not. For, that very moment, a hefty man in dirty clothes came out carrying a huge pan. It was empty, but obviously had some foodstuff – lentil perhaps – that had been cooked in it. He lugged the pan to a tube-well in the by-lane and proceeded to wash it.

No, 'The Lodge' could not be a doctor's clinic at all.

"What is this place?"

Chandan asked at the barber's shop, on one side of the lane. "Is it a clinic?" Razor in hand, the barber laughed out a reply: "Far from it. It's a den of thieves and robbers and old fools."

What was Dadi doing in such a place? The four of them looked at one another. They waited a little and then went forward a few steps. Dadi must not catch them spying on her. They stopped again and waited. It was hot in the by-lane, crowded and uncomfortable. Passers-by were giving them odd glances. Time was ticking by very slowly. They began to feel restive.

"Let's go in and see for ourselves what it is," suggested Bimal.

"Yes, let's do that," agreed Deeksha.

"No," said Anit. "If we come face to face with Dadi, she'll create such a fuss."

"Don't be such a coward," remarked Bimal.

He took a few steps towards 'The Lodge', but stopped.

Dadi had come out! What was more, she was looking at them full in the face. Anit, Bimal, Chandan and Deeksha stood frozen in their positions – as though in a game of 'Statue'.

Then as Dadi began to amble forward to her taxi, they turned and ran towards theirs which was standing a little way off. They reached it in seconds and cried:

"Uncle, start!"

But the taxi-driver had fallen asleep and even when he was jerked out of his sleep, it took him just those few extra seconds to yawn and stretch and then give the vehicle a start.

It was only because of that delay that they heard Dadi's cry. "My bag – my money –"

They whisked around in one movement and saw Dadi fall to the pavement, hitting her head against a lamp-post. At the same glance, they took in that a man in a shiny blue shirt was pushing his way through the by-lane, hurrying off with Dadi's precious leather bag! While Anit and Deeksha rushed to her, Bimal and Chandan made off after the thief.

By the time Anit and Deeksha had reached Dadi, others had gathered around her–passers-by and people from the shops in the lane.

There were cries of 'Get some water', 'What's wrong?', 'Make her sit up', 'Where's she from?' To this, Anit and Deeksha added their cries of "Dadi!"

In a couple of minutes, Dadi had been made to sit up on the pavement itself, leaning against the lamp-post. The barber, who had run out of his shop on hearing Dadi's screams, ran back to his shop for some water and threw the entire mugful on Dadi's face. Unfortunately in his haste, he had got a mug full – not of water – but shaving lather.

Dadi's words – as she came to with a jerk – were words of disgust.

After he had wiped her face with a towel from his shop, and she had cooled down a bit, she came out with what had happened.

"I was just coming along, when this man came from somewhere and gave me a push and snatched my bag away," she said in a shaken voice.

Then her eyes focussed on Anit and Deeksha. With an attempt to return to her old tone of authority, she asked, "And what are *you* doing here?"

Anit and Deeksha looked at each uncomfortably. But they were saved from having to cook up any explanation just then. For, Chandan and Bimal came back, holding between them the man who had made off with Dadi's bag.

He was struggling to free himself and it is doubtful if Chandan and Bimal could by themselves have managed him. But the two taxi-drivers had also come to their aid. "Dadi, we've caught the man who had tried to rob you," shouted Chandan. "And there's your bag, as well," cried Bimal.

"Thank God I had caught sight of the fellow – otherwise, he would have made off to the main road and got lost in the crowd," announced the driver proudly.

The crowd now moved away from Dadi to the taxi.

"*Arrey*, he's Vinod, the jailbird," exclaimed one of the men.

"When did he get out of the jail?" wondered another.

"Let's give him a hiding," was another suggestion.

"Let's take him to the police-station," was yet another.

"Yes, Dadi," said Chandan, "Let's take him there and -"

"– hand him over to the police," Bimal completed the sentence.

"I would just like to go home," said Dadi, her voice tired and faltering.

Chandan and Bimal looked most disappointed, and Anit himself was stunned. Dadi, always so eager to correct, to scold, to punish, was letting a criminal go!

But Deeksha put her arms about Dadi and let her to the taxi. Anit followed the two of them. "They can do what they like, to the man," he heard Dadi say. "I've got my bag back, haven't I?"

"It's as though she is trying to convince herself," he thought. "But why does she not scream and shout and raise hell?"

The man was given a slap or two, and then let off as the crowd began to lose interest in the matter and go back to their own individual affairs. Anit and Deeksha took Dadi home in the taxi she had hired. Bimal and Chandan followed in the one they had taken, as it had to go back to Gurgaon any way.

As their taxi sped home, Anit looked at Dadi's face. With Deeksha's arm round her, she leant back in the taxi, eyes closed. There was a slight swelling on her head where it had struck the lamp-post. There were lines on her cheeks, and circles under her eyes. She looked drained-out, exhausted.

"Why, she's old," thought Anit to himself. "I had never thought of how old she is."

At that precise moment, Dadi opened her eyes and looked at them both. "I don't know what exactly you four were doing in that place," she said, "but I'm glad you were there. And if you don't you tell *Bahu* about this, I won't tell her either."

Dadi acting so mellow? What was wrong?

Broken Bones

Another Sunday!

No particular reason, but today, Anit himself felt like dropping in at the Naths on his way to the park. Bimal came along and joined him.

As he went, he saw Padam, the vegetable-vendor, making his usual morning rounds. Pushing along the card-load of vegetables, he was shouting, "*Sabzi lo! Taza sabzi!*" People were coming up to him to get their vegetables. And, a couple of men were going about with gunny bags, crying '*kabadi*'. Here and there, people stood watching while '*kabadi*' – old newspapers, bottles and tins – were being weighed on scales by the *kabadiwalas*. Autumn sunshine fell cheerfully on the busy neighbourhood.

Gaju was watering the plants as before, with the hose attached to the garden tap.

Water splashed on the rows of plants in front, through Gaju's fingers, which held the mouth of the pipe and turned it here and there.

The garden was coming up quite nicely, commented Bimal. "What a wild mess it was earlier! But then it had belonged to 'us', and now it belongs to `them'."

Was the backyard and the shed too changed? In some sense, Bimal, Chandan and Deeksha had known the back of the house better than the front. It was the back they had used to make their entry into the house. Moving along the passage to the side of the house, they used to get to the back. Then climb in through the broken window of the bathroom at the back. "That window, I wonder if it is repaired by now," said Bimal.

Coming out, they had used the front door. Opening it from inside, then pulling it shut, so that its Yale lock got locked from inside. "It had been easy getting in and out," Bimal's tone was nostalgic.

When Gaju saw Anit and Bimal at the gate, he threw down the hose and went inside the house, possibly to report his coming to Mr. Nath. He was back instantly and called him in with a grin of his big, white teeth.

Gaju led the way, Anit and Bimal followed him through the rooms.

"The house is chockfull of broken things," he thought. Showcases, tables, shelves – all were crowded with antique vases, headless statues, and stone tables with inscriptions. Not a single piece was whole – everything was damaged or disfigured.

"If Mr. Nath is so fond of such things, I don't see why he complained about our breaking a window pane or two!" Bimal muttered to himself.

Gaju led him to the curtained room where the exquisitely pretty lady lay, with Mr. Nath beside her bed. He had the newspaper in his hand.

"She's not letting me leave her side today," explained Mr. Nath. "Else, I would have been waiting for you outside."

Before Anit could say anything, the lady spoke out: "I'm feeling awful today, just awful."

"I know," began Mr. Nath in a soothing voice.

"You don't know, you can't know," complained the lady. "Nobody can know what terrible pains I have."

Mr. Nath sighed.

Anit saw Gaju make a wry face.

"Oh God, I say every day," the lady went on, "Take me up. Gather me up in your bosom. I don't want to live anymore."

"Now, don't say such things," Mr. Nath tried to put in.

But the lady would not stop.

"Oh, that evil day, when I fell down and broke my femur bone! Life ended for me that day," she droned. Then suddenly she broke off in the middle as she caught sight of Gaju standing woodenly, and picked on him. "You rotten fellow, why are you still here? Don't you have any work to do?"

Gaju hung his head and went out. He will find the garden quite flooded, thought Anit. He remembered how Gaju had left the hosepipe lying on the ground.

Mrs. Nath just did not let Mr. Nath have his session with Anit. Mr. Nath tried to seat Anit beside him in the room itself, and read the paper out to him.

But just as Anit would read "Border alert," Mrs. Nath would say, "Fluff my pillow – it's so stiff." Or, as Anit began an Editorial column, she would ask for the window to be closed. "Delhi Unsafe for the Aged," Anit would read, and "Aaah, my leg," she would moan.

After a while, Mr. Nath gave up.

"It's almost ten o'clock now," he said, "Your friends must be waiting for you in the park."

Anit nodded eagerly and stood up.

"I'll give the child some *laddus*," said Mr. Nath, and Anit felt that he took that chance to get away a little.

Hunting for *laddus* in the kitchen, with Anit hanging around, Mr. Nath said, as though to himself: "Poor thing! How she has changed!"

Finding the *laddus*, he handed them to Anit and continued: "One little fall – one little slip – and how everything changes!"

"What had really happened to her?" asked Anit.

"She broke her leg and even though it was re-set, it never healed properly. We were then posted at Tejpur in Assam. A telephone call came and she picked up the receiver and sat down. But she missed the chair by inches and came down upon the floor – hard. We got the best surgeon at Tejpur, but the fracture did not heal. He had made an error and in any case, after a certain age, fractures are difficult to heal. We got the bone re-set by another noted osteopath, but still, she remained an invalid. The best therapist in town could not make her walk. At first, she was cheerful about her misfortune. She thought it would pass. But then it didn't, and she became more and more difficult. She lost faith in doctors. She held *havans* at home. She sought help from *sadhus* and *sants*. She wrote to a friend who had turned a *sannyasin* but she never got a reply. She grew even more depressed. It is not easy to be confined to bed, you know, all the more if you have been a sprinter in your youth."

"Was she one?" Anit asked in surprise.

"Yes, she represented Assam as a sprinter at the national level. She was a sportswoman and in those days, that was quite something." He paused and added, almost shyly, thought Anit: "Love of sports – that is what had brought us together. Remember, I too had been an umpire."

Then they made their way to the front door, through the house full of broken things.

In the Shadows

Next day, Chandan had a doleful face. He could hardly hold his bat straight and got out for a duck.

After the game, he went and sat by himself in one corner of the park. What's eating him, wondered Anit. Usually, their partnership brought in at least a score of runs. But today, it had not worked out. Chandan's mind had not been in the game.

After Anit had got out himself (after scoring 24, no less), he went and accosted Chandan: "What's wrong with you today, *yaar*?"

"It's Chhaya," confided Chandan. "She's no better."

After the match, he accompanied Chandan to his house, which was in the next lane.

Earlier, Chhaya would have recognized their footfalls and flung herself upon the door with joy even as they called out her name.

But for some time now, things had been different.

Chhaya did come up to them, but her walk was laboured, and she sat down almost immediately.

She looked at them with dull eyes.

Chandan told Anit about the time when Chhaya had actually danced with him on her hind legs. She could carry on for at least a minute.

He also told Anit that Chhaya had been with the family for as long as he could remember. She could do 'Shake hand' and fetch balls lightning fast.

Anit looked at the still figure on the floor. "Chhaya, Chhaya!" He called. Very slowly, the tail began to wag, just a little.

"Let us take her to Sharma Uncle," said Anit.

'Sharma Uncle' or Dr. Sharma was the veterinary surgeon who had a clinic not too far away. All the pets of the neighbourhood were under his care.

"No," remarked Chandan gloomily. "I've tried that before."

"Well, let's try again," said Anit.

.

Taking some money from his mother, Chandan called out to Chhaya. She lumbered to her feet, looking expectantly at Chandan.

"Out, Chhaya, out!"

A spark came into Chhaya's eyes and she followed Chandan out of the house. Anit gave a pat on her head and went along with the two of them.

Dr. Sharma's veterinary clinic was beside a big shopping mall with signboards and placards all over it. There were a couple of booths before it, selling momos.

Anit spotted Gaju there, carrying some shopping but at the moment, having momos on the roadside. Gaju too saw him and grinned. "*Amma* wanted tissue and paper napkins and so I had to come here. And I thought, why not have some momos..." His voice trailed off.

"Don't worry, I will not tell her!"said Anit. "Why, he isn't very much older than us," thought he. "But his life is so different."

Outside the veterinary clinic, there was a beautiful black Doberman waiting, along with two fluffy Pomeranians. Chhaya growled when she saw them, but fell silent as they growled back. Inside, a huge Alsatian lay on a steel table, yowling piteously as Dr. Sharma and his assistant gave him a shot. The walls were bright with posters and photographs of dogs of every kind. Multi-coloured collars and leashes hung on a stand, along with steel chains. At another end, there were packets of dog biscuits and bones and teething rings.

Once her turn came, the assistant raised Chhaya on to the steel table and Dr. Sharma examined his patient.

"She's still dull and slow, Uncle," complained Chandan. "She hasn't got better at all."

Dr. Sharma signed for the assistant to get Chhaya down. He spoke in a kindly tone to Chandan: "You better get used to the fact that she won't. I am giving her these pills which you must mix with her food and give her. But they can't work wonders. The fact is that your dog is old and dying."

"But she's only twelve years old," exclaimed Chandan.

"With dogs, that's a pronounced old age," said complained Chandan. "She hasn't got better at all."

Dr. Sharma signed for the assistant to get Chhaya down. He spoke in a kindly tone to Chandan: "You better get used to the fact that she won't. I am giving her these pills which you must mix with her food and give her. But they can't work wonders. The fact is that your dog is old and dying."

"But she's only twelve years old," exclaimed Dr. Sharma.

Anit held on to Chhaya's leash, while Chandan paid the fees and took the pills Dr. Sharma had prescribed for Chhaya. He also bought a big fat bone and some dog biscuits.

Anit knew why. To feel better about Chhaya. But, he also knew that no bone or biscuit would make Chhaya feel better.

"Time's a strange thing," thought he.

On their way back to Chandan's house, they met Padam with his puppy.

It had become mid-day and Padam had finished his rounds. So now, he was taking the puppy along to the vet's clinic for an inoculation that was due. Pappu was so young that he had not finished all his inoculations.

A little bundle of energy, Pappu frisked and frolicked as he went along, and Padam was having quite a job of it.

"Chhaya too had been like that but she never will be again," said Chandan with a catch in his voice.

Chhaya gave him a lick on his hand – as if to comfort him.

Peeping through the Window

Dadi wanted to go out on her own again. Anit could tell so by the fact that she was again making those calculations, and peeping into her leather bag every now and then.

But ever since that mishap, she had been quieter, scolding everybody much less. Perhaps it had given her a jolt. Yes, because this time she asked Anit to accompany her.

"Bimal and the rest can also come along," she added. "I don't mind."

"But Dadi, where? Who is it that you go to see? And why?"

"What is that to you?" Dadi bristled up at once. "Don't poke and pry into the affairs of grown-ups. A child should stay a child."

That was one of her favourite expressions.

But this time, it did not have any effect on Anit.

"Dadi, if you don't tell us what you are about, we won't come with you. Then if people rob you of your precious bag, don't blame us. What is it that is in your leather bag, in any case?"

Dadi clammed up at once. For hours she did not even speak to Anit. But in the evening, she came upstairs as he sat playing computer-games.

She carried a bowl of *mohanbhog* – semolina with *kishmish*, fragrant with *ghee*.

"No one can make *mohanbhog* like you, Dadi," Anit said, as

he took in huge spoonfuls.

"About coming with me –" Dadi began.

"Okay, okay," said Anit.

Ma agreed happily to the idea of Dadi's taking Anit and his friends to the Nehru Planetarium in the precincts of Teen Murti Bhavan. Yes, that was where they told her they were going.

Anit had meanwhile rung up Bimal, Chandan and Deeksha and picked them up in the taxi that had been called for Dadi.

The taxi reached Arjun Nagar and they all got down. Dadi insisted that they stay behind, and they let her have her way.

After she had been gone for about ten minutes, Anit and Chandan went up the by-lane. The barber grinned at them from his shop. He had recognized them. "Take good care of your grandmother," he called out to them.

Anit recalled that last time as they and rushed up to her, they had called out 'Dadi' loudly, many times. That was how he knew.

He grinned back at the friendly barber.

'The Lodge' lay a little ahead. Anit asked the others to stay near the barber's shop and went further ahead, right up to the doorway.

An old man sat dozing at the doorway. His eyes were closed and he did not notice Anit as he sidled along the narrow passage by the side of the building.

There were big windows at the side and Anit looked in through one – the third, it happened to be.

He was looking into a big room where several single beds lay side by side. Some were empty, and some had people lying on them, or sitting. They wore ragged clothes and looked tired and sick. Most of them were grey-haired.

"What business does Dadi have here?" wondered Anit, as he moved over to another window. He gave a start as he looked through this one. For in the room that this window belonged to, there sat Dadi herself, luckily with her back to him.

She was sitting by the bedside of the most peculiar-looking

man he had ever seen. Grey hair, wrinkled skin, robed in star-spangled but old blue cloth with patches on it. An old blue feathered hat. A stick leaning on the bed with a star hanging loosely down from the top.

Why, it was the magician who had given the *kavacha* of Karna to Anit!

Anit ducked to avoid being seen by the man who sat facing the window. The man must have caught a glimpse of him, but thought he was just some kid loitering about. For, he did not raise any hue and cry and instead went on talking to Dadi. Crouched by the window, Anit tried to overhear the conversation.

"So you say that about a lakh is still to left be paid?"

"Yes, well, no. You will have to come out with some more."

"More?" Dadi's voice was pained and sharp.

"*He He He He* –" Anit recognised the laughter that the man broke into.

He raised his head a little and saw the man stretch out his hand, taking something from Dadi. A thick wad of notes. Anit ducked down again. He thought with a shock, "So this is what is in the leather bag! Blackmail dough!"

He could hear Dadi say, "I'll come next week."

"With at least a lakh on you. *He He He He*," laughed the man.

Anit did not hang around anymore. Dadi must not know that he had been shadowing her and had uncovered her guilty secret. He ran out, almost knocking over the old man who still sat dozing at the doorway.

When Dadi came out and looked, she found Anit with the others. They waved at her and after she had come up to them, walked with her to the waiting taxi. There was no mishap today.

"I needn't have brought you along," remarked Dadi after the taxi had started. "What had happened last time was a mere mischance. I shouldn't have let it bother me. Well, I'll have to come here next week as well, but I think I'll come alone – as I used to do."

"We'll see about that," muttered Anit under his breath.

He could barely wait to tell Bimal, Chandan and Deeksha about what he had seen and heard. Dadi seeing in secret the man who had given him the magic talisman! Dadi being blackmailed by a roadside tramp! Bimal, Chandan and Deeksha were also dying to hear him, but Dadi would not leave just then. She would not be a party to an act that was out-and-out deceitful. She declared as follows: "If I have to tell *Bahu* that I took you along to the planetarium, then I must actually take you to the planetarium. As for the rest, let that be."

Well, they did thoroughly enjoy going round the planetarium and the film-show at its auditorium. What a wonder the universe was with its galaxies! In the darkened auditorium, they lost themselves in the infinite that was spangled with stars, planets and asteroids. "It was an asteroid that had hit the earth 65 million years ago and ended the era of dinosaurs," said the commentary. "But for it, human beings may not have been here."

Fare Thee Well

In a couple of days, came Stickler's retirement.

Immaculate and straight as ever, Stickler began addressing the assembly.

"It is with great pride that I look upon you today," he boomed from the dais. Rows and rows of students in shining white uniform stood at attention before him. The teachers, as well as Sanjay the Head-boy and Tarini the Head-girl, stood on the dais with him, tense and erect. The trees too stood still today; not a leaf trembled.

"For years I have tried –patiently and impatiently – for a day when not a single shoelace would be straggling upon the assembly ground. And at last, that day has come. So what if it is the last day of my working years? Better late than never, and I thank you all for at least tying your shoelaces properly in my honour. I am, as you know, a stickler for such details. I joined this school full forty years ago. I was a young man with dreams – I would join the Civil Services. Or perhaps go abroad for further studies. Oh, I had many dreams. All those faded as I began to face reality. The reality of dirty uniforms, running noses, incomplete homework, and bad behaviour of a great variety. The reality of children running wild and undisciplined, not knowing any better. The reality of you. My dreams were gone as I woke up to the reality."

The boy behind Anit poked at him.

"When is he going to get his gift?"

"Right after his address, I guess," whispered Anit.

"Who is it going to give it to him? Sanjay?"

“I guess so,” Anit whispered again. “It can also be Tarini. Now shut up.”

For once, he did not mind listening to Stickler. After all, it was for the last time.

“It was a small school then. Only a hundred students. Only some shacks for classrooms. No building, no playground. And only a young man – that's me–as its Principal. But with time, things changed. Land was acquired in this part of Gurgaon where there were still camels and flocks of sheep to be seen. Gradually, very gradually, a school building rose up. There came to be football grounds, basketball courts, a gymnasium and even a swimming pool. Students were grouped into different ‘houses’ and brought under Head-boys and Head-girls. They began to participate in quiz competitions and declamation contests. Sports-meets and inter-school matches. They began to bring in cups and shields, medals and certificates.

I began to dream different dreams.”

Standing tall and spruce, facing the whole assembly of the staff and students, Stickler went on: “Dreams of opening a further branch. Dreams of having students reaching important positions, winning international recognition, and then coming back proud and glorious to the school's *alumni* meets. Yes, I began to have dreams again. A letter from the school authorities bought me face to face with reality again. The years had gone by and I was an old man who had to retire. I could dream my dreams, but I did not have the time to try and make them come true.”

Out of the corner of his eyes, Anit saw Sanjay whisper something to Tarini. Standing on the dais beside the Principal, as was the school custom, they were looking around for someone. Who? Oh, it was Ranjit, who arrived at the school just then, late. In his hand, he carried a little box, gift-wrapped in silver foil. Anit saw him go forward to Sanjay and Tarini.

The boy behind Anit poked him again. “What's he got with him?”

Anit remembered that Ranjit had taken it upon himself to order the silver replica of the school to be presented to Stickler.

He had obviously collected it himself and had even got it gift-wrapped. Good work! But, of course, it would have been better if he had come a little earlier – on time, that is, and not disturb the entire assembly. For, disturbed it had become. All eyes were now upon Ranjit as he walked up to Tarini, and walked back to the last row of assembled school children.

Stickler frowned at him, but he was in the middle of his speech and did not stop.

"So I leave it to you all to make my dreams come true. I retire. I go. But I leave my dreams with you. They are yours now and you have a long way before your retirement. I have no other words to bid you farewell. This, my message for you today is my farewell to you."

The booming voice fell silent. It was the cue on other days for the children to sing the school song to the beat of the drum. But Sanjay had told them yesterday *not* to start on the school song as soon as Stickler fell silent. Instead, that would be when Stickler would be given his farewell gift.

So when Stickler stopped speaking, Sanjay began.

"Respected Sir, we the students of this school take this opportunity to present you with a small token of our gratitude for the love and care you have bestowed on us all these years."

Anit could hear some titters around him.

"Respected Sir, we know your attitude in this respect. We understand, Sir, that it is grammatically incorrect for *us* to bid *you* farewell. Yet," Sanjay glanced at the chit in his hands, "we feel we just have to give you this little memento – this silver replica of the school building – Oh no!"

The entire school said "Oh no!" in the same breath.

For, as Sanjay had been speaking, Tarini had come forward with the gift and then proceeded to tear off the gift wrapping, open the box, and take out the memento within and hold it high up for everyone to see.

It was shining silver and certainly a good memento.

Only, it was not the replica of any school building, but a stick with a curved handle, the wrong end up.

Stickler's stick and Ranjit's revenge.

Padam and His Puppy

"*Sabzi lo! Taza sabzi!*" As Padam's cry floated in, Ma asked Anit to go out and get some vegetables for her.

"But Ma, I'll be late for school," protested Anit. "Why can't Dadi go?"

"She's at her prayers and I'm making an omelette for Baba. Do this little chore for me, *beta*."

"Oh, all right," said Anit. He had got into his school uniform and had taken up his bag and water bottle. But he knew Ma had a lot to do in the morning.

Taking the money from her, he went out, bag, bottle and all.

A little ahead on the street stood Padam with his wooden cart laden with vegetables, making his regular round of this neighbourhood. Everybody in the neighbourhood knew him, and he knew everybody there.

As Padam was fond of telling his customers, he had started off as a kid accompanying his father, and now he was a man well into his sixties. He had spent almost his entire life pushing his cartload of vegetables with arms that had grown strong and muscular as a result.

His sons had taken up other lines of activity. None of them ever helped Padam with vending the vegetables. But Padam had, he said, no need of them. He was perfectly capable of carrying on by himself.

As Anit went up to Padam, he found that people had gathered around the cart, mostly ladies, feeling the vegetables, loading them into plastic bowls kept for the purpose, passing the bowls to Padam for weighing, and bargaining about the prices.

The puppy, tied to the handle of the cart, was frisking about the wheels.

"No, *bahenji*, that *phulgobi* is not going for less than rupees – Yes, *bahenji*, that's an excellent *lauki* you have chosen –" Padam kept up a steady chatter with his customers, most of them his regulars.

Anit went up to Padam and began to put a few vegetables into a bowl. The puppy jumped about at his feet and he gave it a pat on the head. In delight, Pappu leapt up, and pawed at the handle of the cart. The loop of the rope, with which Pappu had been tied, came off from the handle. Pappu, free from bondage, ran away before anyone could realize anything.

"Just you wait," cried Padam. "I'll catch you soon enough." He bent over his vegetables as the customers pressed on with their various demands.

Anit was turning back with the vegetables he had bought when suddenly there was the roar of a motor-cycle hurtling down the mouth of the lane – going full-speed. The very next instant there was a long-drawn-out squeal. Everybody turned around. A little beyond, at the other end of the road, lay Pappu, with the front wheel of the motorcycle on his quivering body.

Padam dropped the handles of the cart and ran there.

As he picked up the half-dead puppy, he began to shout at the rider of the motorcycle.

"Don't you have eyes in your head? Can't you see where you are going? See what you have done to Pappu!"

"He has all but killed the puppy," shrilled one of the ladies buying vegetables.

"Killer! You are nothing short of a killer!" shouted Padam.

On the motorcycle, there was a young fellow in T-shirts and jeans and a ponytail! There was an expensive-looking video-camera strapped to the back-seat.

He did not look the least bit sorry for his rash and irresponsible driving.

"Shut up, you old man!"he said.

"Why should I?" screamed Padam. "I'll have my say."

"Hold your tongue!" shouted the pony-tailed one and began to start the engine.

One hand clutching the yelping Pappu, the other balled into a fist, Padam lunged towards him. But with a hoot of laughter, the driver reversed the motorcycle and drove back through the mouth of the lane.

Meanwhile, Anit had started to sprinkle Pappu with water from the water-bottle which (luckily, now it seemed) still hung on his shoulder. Muddy and bloody, Pappu continued to squeal pathetically.

"Quick, let's take him to Uncle Sharma," said Anit.

Cartload of vegetables forgotten, Padam hurried to the veterinary clinic with Anit. Only a couple of others accompanied them. Most others went back to their houses, clicking their tongues in idle sympathy. Ma had come out on hearing the commotion, and she shouted out for Anit to stay back.

Anit pretended not to hear.

At the clinic, Sharma Uncle looked grave as he examined Pappu. "I'll clean up its wounds and apply antibiotics," he said. "But it may have suffered severe internal injuries. If the motor-cycle wheel has crushed its intestines, then it's a lost case!"

He put Pappu on a glucose drip. Pappu lay there on the same steel table where a couple of days back Chhaya had lain, looking at the plastic tube going out of his body to the glucose bottle hanging from its stand.

"So you are here," said Ma from the clinic door. She had hurried out after Anit and now she reminded him that he was getting late for school.

Anit did not feel like leaving poor Pappu. But Ma forced him.

School was a little chaotic these days. The new Principal had not yet taken charge, and though the daily activities went on as usual, there was something missing, although Anit could not put his finger on it. There was a layer of dust on the steps – no one had swept them, although they were supposed to have done so by the time school started. Several teachers came to classes late – although they had never done so before. Students jostled one another and chatted loudly in the corridors – although that was strictly against the rules.

A boy, who lived in the same area as Stickler, had brought the news that Stickler had moved out of his house; nobody in the neighbourhood had seen him for quite a few days, whereas he had been difficult to miss otherwise. "Probably gone and hidden his head in shame," he had said. He, as well as most others in the school, had been delighted at the insult handed out to Stickler in the wake of his farewell speech. Most of them had had some grudge against Stickler and Ranjit had become a sort of hero to them in giving it back to Stickler.

Of course, they would have been even more thrilled if Stickler had reacted more openly that day – jumping about on the dais cursing them – or descending upon them waving his stick. But Stickler had done no such thing. He had just gazed at the memento – silently and for a very long time – while the students had tittered loudly and even the staff had covered up their mouths.

Then when the titters had died down, Stickler had looked up from the memento and at the whole assembly. "I thank you all for this thoughtful gift," he had said stiffly. Sanjay, who had recovered himself by then, had gestured for the drums to start beating. Tarini had begun the school song, waving for the assembly to take it up. After that, as was usual, the assembly had broken up and everybody had gone to their classes. They had not seen Stickler again. He must have left for home soon after.

Sanjay, everybody learnt, had not had any inkling of what Ranjit's plan was. He, along with Tarini, had been collecting money from students and that had itself been a big task. So they had been quite glad of Ranjit's offer of dealing with the silversmith.

Even on the day before the farewell, when Ranjit had told him that the silversmith had not finished and would be ready with his work only that evening, Sanjay had not realized that it was Ranjit's way of ensuring that Sanjay never saw the memento beforehand. Unsuspecting, he had happily accepted Ranjit's offer to collect it that evening and bring it to school next morning. Ranjit had come in only at the last moment, with the box gift-wrapped, leaving no scope for Sanjay or Tarini to check it.

Sanjay, Anit gathered from the others, was pretty upset at first. But that had gone when he had realized that no one really blamed him for it. That, in fact, everyone had enjoyed those few minutes of the farewell.

But school was not school without Stickler, felt Anit. Chandan said he felt the same.

They were discussing this as they got down from the school-bus. Then Anit remembered about Pappu and said, "Chandan, *yaar*, let's go to Uncle Sharma's."

"Yes, let's find out about Pappu," agreed Chandan.

They had to turn the corner at the mall in order to reach the vet's clinic. As they approached

the mall, Anit spotted the pony-tailed youth who had run over Pappu. Chatting on the cell phone, cracking jokes and laughing, he was moving towards his motorcycle parked near the clinic.

Anit had told Bimal, Chandan and Deeksha about the incident, and now he pointed him out to Chandan.

Anit and Chandan saw the door of the clinic open and Padam come out. He must have gone to visit his puppy and received some upsetting news. For, as his eyes fell upon the youth, he began to shout again, "Shameless, that's what you are! It's because of you that my Pappu is suffering! And you drive about merrily! Why do you do it? You are not fit for the road. You have no control over your vehicle!"

"Shut your mouth, you old fool!" The pony-tailed fellow yelled back from the motorcycle that he had reached by then.

He started the engine and made a pretence of heading straight at Padam. He stopped just short of ramming into him. “This is what you get for not shutting your mouth!”

Padam lost his balance and fell, but got up dirty and dishevelled. He rolled up his fists.

Anit and Chandan tried to stop ‘Ponytail’.

A few from the gathering crowd also tried to check the youth.

“Hey, let the old man be,” said one of them.

“He’s old enough to be your grandfather!” said another.

Padam dealt Ponytail a blow on the ear. Ponytail seemed stunned. He tottered to the motorcycle and made off.

Padam sat down upon the road with a thump.

“One slap from you one was enough to send him running!” Chandan was surprised. “At your age, that’s quite something.”

Padam grinned. “I am not as old as all that. I can still take care of punks like these.” He flexed the muscles of his bruised arms, “Years of pulling and pushing my cart about – see the result!”

After Padam’s muscles had been duly admired, Chandan brought him a cold drink from a stall in the cinema-hall. Anit asked him about Pappu. “He’s not dead – is he?”

“No, but Sharmaji said he cannot say anything for sure.”

Padam looked so sad that Anit felt he must say something to cheer him up. “Don’t worry,” he said. “It’s your puppy and it’ll be as spirited as you. It won’t give up the fight easily.”

“Yes,” Chandan supported him. “It’ll live up to a ripe old age, like you.”

Padam looked pleased.

“Go home now, and put some ointment on your hurts,” advised Anit.

“Yes, I need some rest,” admitted Padam. He moved away, dragging his feet a little.

Chandan and Anit went to the clinic to take a look at Pappu.

Old Connections

Next Sunday, Anit found Mr. Nath sitting in the front garden, with the newspaper on a stool beside his own chair. Mrs. Nath must be less grumpy today, he thought.

With the advent of autumn, the rose-bushes in the garden had broken out into buds. Dahlias and chrysanthemums were coming up as well. As before, Gaju was there with a hosepipe.

Gaju took good care of the garden. Watering the plants, trimming their branches, digging and spraying among the roots. Bimal, Chandan and Deeksha admitted that Gaju had completely changed the look of the place. What a wilderness it had been only last winter when they had had it at their disposal.

Anit started reading out the headlines one by one.

"Plane Crash in High Altitudes," "Whole Family Hacked to Death," and so on. When he came to "Cricketer of Yesteryears Dies," there was a sharp intake of breath.

Anit could not even recognise the name but Mr. Nath were clearly moved.

At Anit's surprised glance, he said, "You haven't heard of him? That's what time does to you."

He made Anit read out the obituary.

"In the sixties, he had been quite a phenomenon. I remember the flash of his bat at Eden Gardens," recalled Mr. Nath, his dull, grey eyes beginning to shine. "I remember how handsome he had looked that day! You know, the girls used to run after him like anything! Why, even Mrs. Nath was a fan of his!"

Anit almost laughed at this, but Mr. Nath sounded perfectly serious.

"Well, he has died at the age of 70, in Bangalore, where he had been leading a quiet life for the last decades. He is survived by two sons and four grandsons."

"Grandsons!" Mr. Nath said to himself. "Somehow it is difficult to think of him with grandsons. You see, whenever I think of him, I see that wiry young fellow with stroke after stroke coming from his bat."

"Do you have any grandsons of your own? Or, well, sons?" Anit suddenly asked him.

"Of course I do!" came the reply. "Two, just your age!"

"Then why can't they read out the paper to you?" The question was out before Anit had realized he was going to ask it. Mr. Nath's face blanched. The light went out of his eyes and left them dull and grey once more. For seconds, he could not utter a word but just sat looking blankly at Anit.

Then, with a sigh, he said softly, "Why indeed!"

There was silence for a while and Anit felt rotten that he had asked his question. "Have you shown your eyes to an occult – occul – well," Anit hesitated for a moment, not sure of the exact word. "Well, an eye-doctor?" he said in the end.

"Yes, child, and he told me that I have got cataract in my eyes."

"What's that?" asked Anit, vaguely remembering Dadi too using the word.

"It's something that age brings as a must – a film over the eyeballs. You can get rid of it only by undergoing an eye-operation."

"Why don't you – well, undergo it then?" asked Anit enthusiastically.

"I'm scared," said Mr. Nath with a sigh.

"Scared?" Anit was surprised.

"Supposing it doesn't turn out right? Supposing I lose my

sight completely? It's happened to people I know. Oh, they say eye surgery is very easy these days – with lasers and things. But it's still a risk and I am plain scared. Not for myself," Mr. Nath hastened to say, "but for that bedridden creature there. Who will take care of her if by chance I get completely blinded?"

Again there was silence. Anit could not think of a single thing to say. He was relieved when just at that point a thin cry came floating from the house.

"Have both of you gone quite deaf? I have been calling out for over an hour."

Mr. Nath got up and hurried inside, and so did Gaju.

Anit sat there, not knowing what to do. Then Gaju came out, telling him he could go off. Paper-reading was over for that day.

There was a nip in the air. Woollens had come out of their plastic bags, smelling of naphthalene. At the park, Anit found all his friends in light woollens. Bimal, in particular, was looking rather unhappy in a sweater half his size.

"New pinch," said Deeksha and pinched Bimal hard.

"Don't you do that," growled Bimal "I hate it."

"But it's a new sweater," remarked Deeksha. "I have never seen it before."

Seeing one another almost every day, they were familiar with one another's wardrobes.

"It is new enough," said Bimal. "My *Nani* had sent it last week. *Nani* always sends me things that don't fit. I look such a fool in them. But I have to go round in them, and what is more, I have to write letters to *Nani* thanking her for them, saying that they fitted me fine."

"Why Bimal?" asked Chandan.

"Oh, Mom says it would hurt her feelings otherwise. You see, she sends me something hand-knitted almost every year. She loves knitting. It's a thing with her. But she gets to see me only once in a while. She knits them from her memory of me on my last visit or from the photographs Mom sends her. So her sweaters and stuff never really fit me. And yet, Mom thinks she will be hurt if I tell her so."

"But why does she get to see you only once in a while?" asked Anit.

"Because she lives quite far away – in a village in the interior of Orissa – the village Mom comes from. She married her daughter – that's Mom – to Dad, who's completely Delhi-based. So she does not get a chance to see her – or me – very often. I have gone to that village a couple of times, once when *Nanaji* died, and once when we went for a holiday to Gopalpur-on-sea. But Dad says it is difficult to keep going there whenever Mom wants to."

Bimal's words set Anit's thoughts on a different track altogether. Did Mr. Nath's grandsons too stay far away from him?

Perhaps Mr. Nath's sons lived in Madurai or Surat or Tejpur or some remote place? Perhaps they lived abroad – in the USA, the UK or the UAE?

"Come on, let's start," called Chandan, who had been busy all this while setting the wicket. And Mr. Nath's grandsons were forgotten.

But later in the day, at home, Anit could not help thinking about it. Evening was falling. In the sitting room, the television was on. Some political personality was airing his views on the nation's future. Baba was intently watching it, whereas Ma was asking him to change the channel. She had finished part of her housework and wanted to relax a little before she got up to do the rest. Dadi sat on the divan, lost in her own thoughts.

"I wonder where Mr. Nath's grandsons are!" remarked Anit suddenly.

"Who is Mr. Nath and why are you bothered about his grandsons?" queried Dadi.

"Oh, Mr. Nath is Anit's new friend," Ma's smile was teasing.

"A man who has grandsons – Anit's friend?" Dadi raised her eyebrows.

So Anit had to tell her all about Mr. Nath, right from the very beginning.

As he went on, Dadi began to frown, as if trying to remember something. When he mentioned the beautiful old lady who had run for Assam at the national level, Dadi sat up with excitement.

"Why, that sounds like our Meera! I was at school with her!"

Anit gave a start. Dadi a schoolgirl! That was so difficult to imagine. Mrs. Nath, her school friend! That too was difficult to imagine. But Dadi was insisting on more and more details and getting more and more convinced that Mrs. Nath was her childhood friend Meera.

"Yes, now I remember I had heard that Meera had got married to the curator of a museum in Nepal, who was also an amateur umpire. I myself was getting married then and moving over to Patna. I lost all touch with her. To think that now she's almost next door!"

This prattle went on for quite some time. Baba was refusing to change the channel and let Ma watch a TV serial she was fond of watching and which was due in minutes. So Ma too was drawn into Dadi's conversation.

"Tell me, has Meera still got long hair up to her waist? You know, *Bahu*, she had such lovely hair! It was so long that it came up to her ankles. Once she had even tripped up on her long plaits. We had all laughed but also felt envious. You don't see hair like that these days! No wonder short hair is in vogue."

Ma, who had only shoulder-length hair, looked embarrassed.

"And not only her hair, Meera's eyes, her complexion, her walk; everything about her was wonderful. Well, but for her voice perhaps, which was rather thin and carrying." Dadi paused and then continued, "She was so vivacious, our Meera, so full of life. Never could sit still for a moment. Always running about and laughing. Well, a bit impatient perhaps of anything that did not suit her, a little too critical. But in the Annual Sports, she won every single race. Not only the 100 metres and 200 metres, but the one-legged-race, the sack race, everything! She became the State champion and did quite well at the national level as well. But then she went to college, made new friends, met this curator who was also a sports-enthusiast –got married to him – and that is the last

I heard of her."

As Anit had guessed, the next thing she wanted was to go over to the Naths at once.

"*Bahu*, get up and come with me," she commanded imperially.

Ma did not want to go visiting just then, as Anit could make out from her expression. He tried to make Dadi a bit more reasonable.

"Dadi, there's absolutely no guarantee that she is actually that Meera of yours. Let me make sure before you go over."

"Oh, I can't wait to see Meera," Dadi's voice was eager like a schoolgirl's.

In the end, Anit had to offer to take her to the Naths. He felt Ma should be allowed to see her favourite TV serial – especially as Baba had finally agreed to change the channel.

The Flight Of Time

Mr. Nath was certainly puzzled to see Anit and Dadi at his gate. But he sent Gaju out to unlock the gate. It was the custom in this suburb to lock the gates as soon as it began to grow dark. On several occasions, there had been burglaries, at least, attempted ones. The Residents' Welfare Society had organized a neighbourhood watch system, but it was not very effective. In the nights, people did hear the watchmen going about striking the ground with their sticks. But in the afternoons or evenings, there were hardly any watchmen about. Instead, the residents locked their gates and were pretty careful about opening them.

Once Gaju had unlocked the door, Anit led Dadi across the garden. At the front door stood Mr. Nath, with an uncertain smile on his face.

"This is my Dadi," said Anit. "And the reason why she's come with me is that –"

He fumbled for the right way to put the whole thing before Mr. Nath, but before he could go on, Mrs. Nath's voice rang out from her bedroom.

"Gaju, who is it at this time of the day? Who has come to disturb us?"

"That's Meera's voice!" cried Dadi.

"Yes, of course," faltered Mr. Nath. "But how do you know that?"

Without bothering to explain herself, Dadi shouted, "Meera? Meera, where are you? It's Champa!"

Anit gave a start. Champa? Could Dadi possibly have a name like Champa?

Mr. Nath had quickly taken in the situation. He politely asked Dadi to come along with him to Mrs. Nath's bedroom. Anit followed, along with Gaju.

Raising the thick curtain, Dadi rushed into the bedroom.

Then she stopped petrified as she caught sight of the figure on the bed.

Mrs. Nath gazed at Dadi – "Champa!" she said in a whisper, as recognition crept into her eyes. She tried to raise her body as if to get up to meet Dadi but sank back on her pillow immediately. A wan smile appeared at the corner of her lips, and at the same time the tears spilled out.

Anit watched as Dadi tottered to the chair at the bedside, and sank down into it.

This was one occasion when Dadi had no words to say. Or, even if she had, she could not get them out of her throat. She just sat by the bedside of her old friend, silently, as the room grew dark and the evening passed into night, also silently.

Finally, it was Mrs. Nath who put out a wrinkled hand on Dadi's own, and said, "Time, it's all the doing of time."

"Yes. It's so much stronger than us," agreed Dadi.

Then they started to talk – and once they had started, they could not stop.

Words came tumbling out of them. Questions popped out one after the other. Interrupting each other, flitting from one query to another, they went on – to Anit it seemed for hours.

At Mr. Nath's order, Gaju had brought in some tea and biscuits for Dadi. But she didn't touch them, so taken up was she in chatting to her long-lost friend. It was Anit who stood beside her and munched the biscuits and listened to the endless chatter. Mr. Nath was also listening from a chair in the corner of the room.

"Remember how plump you were at school, Champa?" asked Mrs. Nath.

"I still am," laughed Dadi. "I was never the beauty that you were."

"What use is beauty without luck, Champa? Look at me now, tied to the bed all day. You are at least up and about."

"Yes, I've got to be grateful for that. But tell me, Meera, what children have you got? I have got one son, and he is in Patna. This child here belongs to a nephew, and that nephew is also like a son to me. I stay in Patna with my son, but every year, I come to Delhi to stay with my nephew. Well, this time it is Gurgaon because my nephew has shifted here."

Dadi went on. "While I am in Patna, I have to run my son's household. And when I am in my nephew's household, I take charge of his." Dadi beamed, "I don't mind, actually. I like pottering about the house. You remember, I was never much interested in studies, or sports, for that matter. Good thing that my parents got me married early."

"When did you lose your husband? What had he been like?"

Descriptions of his dear departed grand-uncle followed. All his good points were listed, along with his bad ones (playing bridge, being careless about money, and not listening to Dadi).

From the looks cast in Mr. Nath's direction, Anit could make out that Mrs. Nath really wanted him to go, so that she could air her views about him to Dadi. But as Mr. Nath sat there stolidly, she could not. "You haven't told me about your children, Meera," Dadi said at the end of her faithful account of her late husband.

"Oh, there are two of them. Both settled abroad. Narender, that's the elder one, is in Boston, USA, and Birender, the younger one, is in Dublin, Ireland." In a voice of deep pride, she added: "Both my *bahus* are golden-haired and blue-eyed. So are my grandsons and there are four of them." Dadi wanted to see their photographs but Mr. Nath interrupted. "You are talking too much, Meera, and getting yourself overstrained. There's tomorrow as well and the day after – your friend is not running away."

"That's true, Champa, come tomorrow. You must come tomorrow itself, Champa, there's such a lot to talk about."

Dadi had taken Mr. Nath's hint and got up. Why, she too is looking tired, thought Anit. Well, it was almost dinner-time now. Night had fallen.

Dadi caressed Mrs. Nath's silvery hair. "Of course I'll come tomorrow. I'll come every day while I'm here."

She turned to go and had raised the curtain when Mrs. Nath shot out another question at her. "How's Houdini? I almost forgot to ask."

Anit saw Dadi stiffen and cast a glance at her.

"Tomorrow, all that is for tomorrow," she stalled the question and went out.

Mr. Nath accompanied them to the gate and spent some time giving Dadi details of what exactly had happened to Mrs. Nath.

Then, as he locked the gate and went in, Dadi and Anit began to walk home. It was a quiet neighbourhood, although only a little ahead lay the mall and the busy main road. The air was chilly, and Dadi wrapped her shawl close. To Anit, she said, "Walk fast, or you will catch a cold. You should have brought something warm along."

She was about to start scolding, when Anit asked, "Dadi? Who's Houdini?"

Dadi did not answer, but walked on.

"Who's the Houdini she was asking about? I have never heard you take that name!"

Their house came and yet, there was no reply from Dadi.

Ma was at the door, full of queries. Dadi was just as eager to tell Ma all about the visit.

Anit could not get in a word edgeways.

Anyway, it was almost dinner-time and he was ravenous. He went to the dining table to look into the casseroles.

Washing One's Dirty Linen

Dadi went over to the Naths the very next day, and the next and the next. The entire week, she never missed a day. She told Ma about her visits in great detail, regretting every day that Meera had not located her family album. But to Anit's queries about 'Houdini', she did not break her silence.

Bimal, Chandan and Deeksha (whom Anit had lost no time in telling everything) agreed with Anit that Houdini could only be the name of the man who had sold him the magic talisman.

"What a name – Houdini," exclaimed Anit.

"Houdini is the name of a great magician," Deeksha had Google-searched. He could make escape acts from impossible circumstances and places, even under handcuffs and under water. In 1912, he invited the press to watch as he was put in handcuffs and leg-irons, nailed into a crate roped and weighed down with two hundred pounds of lead, which was then lowered into East River, New York. He escaped in less than a minute while the crate remained intact with the chains inside.

"Impossible, *yaar*, I don't believe it!" exclaimed Chandan. "People had actually seen Houdini work his magic," said Deeksha."Then it must be mass-hypnotism," said Chandan.

"But, the question is," said Bimal, "What can Dadi have to do with him?"

"Nothing," remarked Deeksha calmly. "For, Houdini was a

Hungary-born American, born in 1874 and dead since1926. It's another man nicknamed Houdini that Dadi has something to do with."

Bimal made a face at her.

Houdini remained a mystery.

Meanwhile, Pappu survived the accident and was again on the rounds with Padam. The accident had endeared the little thing to Anit and Chandan, and Chandan had even gifted Pappu a warm coat with straps at the bottom.

It had once belonged to Chhaya who had outgrown it.

When Padam vended the vegetables in the neighbourhood, Pappu came along prancing in Chhaya's hand-me-down. Chandan liked to see that.

At school, summer uniforms had been replaced by winter ones. Stickler had been most particular about blazers. Every button must shine. None should be loose and dangling at the end of threads. The emblem on the pocket must not look crumpled. But the Acting Principal Mr.Jalan did not bother.

This morning, as Anit walked to the bus stop with Chandan, he noticed Chandan's shirt-collar was dirty and his blazer crushed.

In Stickler's days, this would have been unthinkable. Chandan would rather have been marked absent than risk being seen by Stickler in this state. But not only did he venture out to school today, but seemed quite unconcerned about his appearance.

Still, something must be wrong, and Anit asked what it was.

"Mom's not here, you see. Usually, it's she who sees to it that my uniform's in order."

Anit said proudly "Ever since Class Six, I have looked after my own uniforms. I've even learnt to wash and press them."

"Where's Aunty gone off to?" he asked after a while.

"Day before yesterday she received a call from Durgapur. *Nanaji*'s had a stroke. So Mom had to rush off." Anit was about to say something polite and sympathetic, when Chandan blurted out angrily, "*Nanaji*'s always having these strokes. He's had two earlier."

"*Yaar*, what an awful thing to say! Don't you feel bad for him?"

"Anit, I've seen just him a couple of times. How bad can you feel for someone you don't know?"

Anit nodded his head slowly. He knew it was awful, what Chandan was saying. But was it entirely untrue? He did not know what exactly to say.

Ah, there came the school bus, a little late these days, unlike in Stickler's time, when it had arrived every day on the dot. It had not mattered for the first two days. All the children who availed of the school bus had got some extra time to chat at the bus stop. But then it became boring and everyone began to get irritated at the delays.

So now when the school bus came into sight, both Anit and Chandan gave a sort of cheer. They were getting into the bus, when there came the roar of a motorcycle. There Ponytail was. "What is he doing around here?" asked Chandan. "Just hanging around, I guess," said Anit. The motorcycle came into the lane at high speed. Went right up to its end, and then turned an abrupt U. With a screech and a growl, it was gone again.

The bus-driver shouted out at him and then gave a start to the bus.

At school there was big news – the new Principal was coming the next day!

Their class-teacher, Madam Paramjeet, announced it herself at the break, confirming the rumours floating around the school since morning. "He's extremely learned and most scholarly and very young as well!" She informed them. "Mind it, you have to be on your best behaviour before him."

The Acting Principal, Mr. Jalan, ordered all the caretakers and cleaners to spruce up the school. "No child should appear in uniform that is dirty or crumpled," he announced. "We must make a good impression before the new Principal. You see, he's young and will be the Principal of this school for years and years.

It's important that he forms a good impression of the school." He cleared his throat and added, "We have been a bit slipshod of late, but none of that tomorrow."

This announcement made Chandan rather worried.

All the way home, sitting beside Anit, he grumbled, "Trust Mom to have gone off just now. Trust *Nanaji* to have his stroke just now. Trust the new Principal to come just now."

Irritated, Anit gave him a shove and he fell off his seat on to the floor of the bus, ruining the seat of his trousers. He got up and gave Anit a tight slap. Anit, tired after the day at school, aimed a punch at Chandan's nose. The bus-driver, sensing the disturbance at the back, bellowed out for them to behave themselves or he would drive the bus into the traffic-light. Chandan and Anit calmed down, Chandan still looking gloomy.

The bus went along its usual route, stopping and dropping children at its usual stops. The area where Chandan and Anit lived drew near. They sat in the emptying bus, still cross with each other. Then as the familiar bus-stop drew near, Anit said, "Shall I help you with your uniform?"

"Will you?" exclaimed Chandan, brightening up at once. They got down from the bus, the best of friends.

At home, Ma was not so pleased with the idea of Anit's going over to Chandan's to help him out.

"It'll be simpler if you just bring his things along and let me see what I can do about them, "she said.

However, Dadi backed Anit. "No, no. Let the kid go. *Bahu*, never discourage kids when they want to do something for themselves."

"She doesn't," Anit wanted to say. "It's Ma who has taught me how to wash and press my own uniform."

But Dadi had already started off. She gave a short lecture on the virtues of self-help, and then another on those of friendship. Anit could only listen – as he munched the tiffin Ma had put on the dining table for him – hot *bread-pakoras* with tomato sauce (home-made in Dadi's honour). Then he gulped down the milk, and with a quick 'Bye', went off to Chandan's.

It was good to see Chhaya, though she seemed to be no better. Earlier, she would have tried to join in anything the two of them were up to. Today, after the initial wagging of tails, she went and lay down in her corner. Uncle – Chandan's father – had just returned from office. He rang up for some pizza to be delivered home. Anit and Chandan started their business with the shirt and the blazer.

Every washing machine has its own personality, so has every toaster, mixer-grinder, iron or vacuum cleaner. Every machine is different – no two ever have the same traits. Anit had known this, but he was not prepared for the eccentricities of the washing machine in Chandan's house. He had to spend a whole hour persuading it to clean up and dry Chandan's shirt. Then there was the task of ironing the shirt and the blazer as well. Finally, it was over and when Anit left (after tucking into slices of the home-delivered pizza), it was with a sense of satisfaction.

But it had grown cold and dark. Chandan's father offered to drop Anit home. Anit laughed off the idea. His house was just down the lane – just a few minutes' walk. Nevertheless, he gave a big start as he caught sight of a man hanging around in front of their house. As the man realized Anit was heading for that house and no other, he moved away. All Anit could see was that he was heavily wrapped up in a shawl. And that he wore something shiny underneath the shawl, parts of which were showing.

He told Ma and Baba about it and they were a little alarmed.

"We must double-check the locks before we got to sleep," remarked Ma. "Every day, the newspapers report some burglary or the other."

"Be on the lookout and tell us if you see the man again," added Baba. "I must report the matter to the Residents' Welfare Society. This area of ours is becoming more and more crime-prone."

Dadi launched into an account of how safe and secure life had been when she had been a child. "We never even bothered to lock our doors at night ..."

"But the story you used to tell me about how burglars took away all your mother's jewellery!" remarked Anit.

"Oh that –" said Dadi, faltering a little. "That was —-"

"All cooked up, wasn't it?" taunted Anit, "Just to make me go to sleep?" He felt tired and angry. He had – not too much in the past – been rather fond of that story.

A Lift

As luck would have it, the next day Anit happened to miss the school-bus, and Baba had to drive him to school. "Why didn't you get up on time?" He scolded as he drove on. "You got late yourself and now you are going to make me late for office as well!"

A schoolboy thumbed at the car for a hitch.

Baba gave a grunt of disapproval and pressed on the accelerator. "I hate people hitching – especially when I'm in a hurry. And precisely when I am in a hurry – that's now – or coming back from office – there they stand – thumbing at me."

He ignored several such thumbs, but finally had to admit defeat.

A spectacled young man, with hair dishevelled and brand new suit all awry, appealed frantically at a red light.

"It's an important occasion for me today, Sir, can you please give me a lift–– you are headed that way, Sir, I can see – It will be awful if I'm late – "

"I guess it's an interview," Baba said with a sigh of resignation.

He opened the door of the car and let the man drop into the seat next to his.

Anit knew that Baba hated people 'hitching' as much as he hated people sitting next to the driver's seat and chatting. But the fellow they had taken in kept up an incessant chatter. With barely a glance at Anit who sat at the back, he plunged into the story of his life.

He told Baba all about his hometown, his family, and the various educational institutions he had attended, and the various places where he had been refused jobs. His name was Neogi.

From time to time, he passed his hands through his unruly hair, and Anit noticed that he had the habit of biting his nails.

As it was getting to be office-hour, there was a lot of traffic about. Baba had to stop several times at red-light stops. He tapped his fingers on the steering wheel impatiently, but there was no respite from the steady stream of words that came from the young man beside him.

"I wanted to join the Civil Services, and I even made it to the Interview. But then things went wrong and in any case, I would have got disqualified at the medical examination. My eyes are bad, you know," he confided in Baba, squinting at him through his thick glasses.

"I wanted to go abroad, Sir, and took the GRE and TOEFL. The TOEFL was okay, but my GRE scores were too low. I have been a topper, Sir, in all my exams. But that GRE, I really could not tackle it. Have you ever taken the GRE, Sir?"

"No, I have not," remarked Baba shortly. "Where exactly would you like to be dropped? Where is your interview to take place?"

"Interview?" Mr. Neogi stared.

Meanwhile, the lights had changed and the car was speeding along Sohna Road.

From the distance, they could see the familiar school-building. Anit could also see a couple of school-buses taking the roundabout. That meant he would not be too late for school. Baba would be sure to reach school within minutes of those buses, and Anit would enter school more or less the same time as the other bus-travelling children. It was most important not to be late today, with the new Principal addressing the Assembly.

"Yes, tell me where your interview is scheduled to take place?" Baba repeated his question, as he took the roundabout. ,

"But I don't have any interview today," said Mr. Neogi,

looking bewildered. "I've already been selected."

"For what, may I ask?" asked Baba with chilling politeness. "Which company – which institution has made such an error of judgment?"

"It's this school, Sir, just over there. You can see that building where those buses have lined up. I am a nephew of the Chairman of its Governing Body, and so they removed the age bar and took me in. I don't know if I'm at all the right person, Sir. If you ask me, I'm quite scared of handling all those kids in there. My stomach's churning at the thought, and I've got a weak stomach, Sir, you know. Oh God, I wish I didn't have to address this Assembly that they have at the school. Oh God, I wish I had never been selected."

"I can honestly say I reciprocate your feelings," remarked Baba with a straight face, as he drew up the car behind the school-buses, and opened the door for the young man to get out. The man looked taken aback at Baba's comment, but as he saw Anit get down and peered at the emblem on his blazer, the truth dawned upon him and his jaw fell open. All Anit could do was not to burst out laughing in his face.

Under Cover Of Darkness

Night had fallen. Dinner was over. Dadi had gone to bed. Baba and Ma were watching television. As it was Saturday, Anit did not have to get up early next morning. He was in high spirits.

Assembly at school had been like no other Assembly before. The new Principal had hemmed and hawed and finally come out with a speech nobody could hear because of its low, trembling tones.

Sanjay and Tarini had managed the situation, because the titters had risen higher and higher as the speech had gone on.

The staff members had looked at one another. Anit had seen Madam Paramjeet smile and Mr.Jalan frown.

The children had all been disgusted. But Chandan had been particularly so.

"To think of how we spent all last evening washing and pressing clothes because he was coming today!" he kept on saying. "To think what fools we were!"

On the journey back, when he sat next to Anit in the bus; that is the refrain he kept up.

"It's only the first day," said someone from the seat ahead.

But that did not calm Chandan down. "It's the first day that counts," he said. "Morning shows the day."

Well, if morning did show the day, there were odd times ahead of the school. But perhaps the situation would change in a couple of days, as Principal Neogi found his feet, although Anit thought that unlikely. Anyway, there was nothing to do but to wait and see. Meanwhile, no one was referring to the new Principal as Mr. Neogi. He was simply being called Neo.

Leaving Baba and Ma to watch television, Anit went up to the study, played some computer-games, and then came out to the tiny balcony attached to this room. This next moment, he was clattering down the stairs.

"Baba, look out, there's that man again."

Both Baba and Ma rushed to the sitting-room window.

Yes, they too saw him. A figure swathed in a shawl, standing in the shade of their house, and looking around. The neighbourhood was pretty well-lit, yet he had chosen a shady portion to stand in.

"Here, listen, what do you want?" Baba called out in Hindi. "Why are you here, standing?"

The man started, looked up, and with a flash of something shiny under his dark shawl, turned and ran. Anit was rushing down to follow him. But Ma held him back. Baba too said that there was no need to go after him. The man was a suspicious character all right, loitering about the neighbourhood, watching for opportunities of housebreaking. The proper way to tackle him would be to inform the Residents' Welfare Society about him and get the night watchman alerted.

They must have been talking quite loudly. For, Dadi came out of her room with a questioning look. "I must tell Meera about it the first thing tomorrow," she declared.

Anit went to bed, but could not fall asleep at once. He kept seeing the man huddled in the shawl, standing in the shade, watching and waiting, and then running away with a flash of something that shone. A terrible thought struck him. Could it be Ponytail? After all, he had been hanging around the place. Perhaps he had a grudge against Anit and had found out which house he lived in, to keep watch on him. Perhaps he was looking for a chance to get at him.

But then, he remembered with a start, it could also be Vinod-the-jailbird. He had not been able to rob Dadi of her bag. But if that area was a regular haunt of his, he might have spotted Dadi (and Anit) on the subsequent visit, and followed her here hoping to get his hands on her bag sometime or the other.

Or perhaps the man had no particular link with anyone or anything in the area but was just on the lookout for a suitable house to rob.

None of the thoughts were comforting. Under cover of darkness, what was the man planning to do?

Anit had taken off his talisman at Ma's command. But now he put it on again. He felt he needed it.

Caught!

Dadi did not, however, go to her friend the first thing in the morning. Instead, she came to Anit, even as he lay lolling on his bed.

She ran her fingers through Anit's curls and it felt lovely. But Anit knew Dadi's ways. "What is it, Dadi? What do I have to do?"

Dadi's fingers did not stop travelling amongst Anit's curls, but she said, "Well, I was thinking of going along to –"

"To where, Dadi?" Anit sat up on the bed in indignation, throwing Dadi's hand off. "You want us to come along with you, isn't it? You are not so sure of yourself now. And you do want us to be with you. But you won't tell us where you are going and why. Well, let me tell you something. The deal's off. Unless you let us into your secret, we refuse to go along with you. And what's more, we will go and tell everybody what you have been up to, mixing with criminals and jail-birds and being blackmailed."

There was silence. Dadi sat staring at Anit, not uttering a single word.

"You have to tell me, Dadi, and you have to tell me at once." Anit was red in the face. "Unless you begin, I'm going downstairs and waking Baba up. What do you think he'll say when he finds out about your dealings with the underworld? Will you be able to look him in the face after that?"

"The underworld!"To his utter astonishment, instead of grovelling at his feet as he had expected Dadi to do, she burst into laughter. She laughed and laughed till tears ran out of her old eyes and she had to wipe them.

Then she sat up and said in a business-like tone, "I will tell you all about where I have to go, and why. But not today, Annu, my little one. Well, I see you are no longer a little one, and I promise I won't keep things a secret from you and Bimal and the rest. But let me be today. I'm already in a state of worry today, especially after I saw h–well – he whom you all saw last night."

Anit rang the others up. But none of them could come along. In fact, they said that they would not even be able to come out to play in the park that morning. Bimal was being taken to meet an uncle in Ghaziabad. Deeksha was being taken to meet an aunt in Faridabad. Chandan had been ordered to stay at home in case his mother rang up with some urgent message (which Chandan would then communicate to his father who always slept late on Sundays).

So around 9 in the morning, it was just the two of them in the taxi.

Dadi had taken her leather bag along. Anit wondered what it contained. He leaned against it and there was a tinkle from inside. Now, what could that be?

"Wait here in the taxi while I go up," said Dadi trustingly and went forward. After a margin of some five minutes, Anit followed. Waving a greeting to the friendly barber, he went forward to 'The Lodge' and once again dodging the sleepy old man at the doorway, sidled up to the window on the side.

"Why did you do such a foolhardy thing yesterday?" Anit heard Dadi's voice. "What was the need?"

"I did nothing yesterday – I was here all the time."

"I saw you outside the house – in your blue robe that you will never throw away."

"It wasn't me, Champa."

"I can't believe that. Why else had you taken the address the last time?"

"It wasn't me yesterday – take it or leave it – *He He He He.*"

There rang out the laughter that Anit had heard on earlier occasions.

Dadi's voice again. "Didn't you know that I would have come today? Don't you have that much faith in me?"

"I have no faith in anyone," was the reply. The voice was old and dry and Anit recognized it to be the voice of the personality he had glimpsed last time. "I have lost all trust in humankind."

"That's because you have never kept *your* trust with humankind. Never been steady in your pursuits."

"I have also had the most rotten of luck...Tell me, hadn't it brought me bad luck, those necklaces and bangles of our mother that I made off with? I sold them, I pawned them, but whatever I got, I always lost."

So Dadi had not entirely made up that story Anit loved to hear.

Dadi's voice was a little softer as she said: "You have never told me the details."

"Well, I bought my plane ticket to Hungary with some of that money. It was the land where my master, my hero, had been born. But it was a wasted trip. There was no one there who was worth the name of my hero. I did pick up a few tricks here and there, and tried to survive by showing whatever magic I knew, but with the Second World War coming on, who had time for roadside shows? It cost a lot to survive there – with Europe at war – and when it was over, the world had changed. Besides the marvels of modern technology, magic had become a faded, old thing. There was no glamour in it and no money either."

So the man was a professional magician? Reduced to a peddler of charms and talismans? Of course! Anit remembered the spangled blue dress, the turban and the wand he had seen last time. It must have been that robe that the man had worn underneath the shawl. That would explain the flash that had caught Anit's eyes as the man had moved away.

"Why didn't you forget about it and turn your hand at something useful?" Anit heard Dadi ask.

The man's tone hardened immediately. "I knew you would say such a thing, Champa. That is why I say nobody's ever understood me, not even my own people. How could I give up magic? It's my life. It's all I have ever lived for."

"It ruined your life, that's what I think," replied Dadi with spirit. "What is more, it broke mother's heart and father's too."

"As if he had a heart, Champa. He was the hardest man there ever was."

"That's what you think, but he really took it hard – you running away from home."

"Is that why he had disowned me publicly? Cut me off from his will? Forbidden you to have any connection with me?" The old man shot out the questions like bullets from a gun.

They must have pierced Dadi's heart. For, she answered in a very soft voice: "Let all that be. I nursed him at his deathbed. I know his last thoughts were of you."

"Much use that has been to me," said the man.

"You are incorrigible," Dadi's voice hardened. "Anyway, I have brought you all I had left. I would have brought cash if I had got some more time to sell them off. But when I realized it must have been you yesterday, I hurried here with the things unsold. If you can't possibly wait, then you will have to sell them yourself."

"*Arrey*, going so soon?"

"You know I'll come again. Only, don't go there yourself. They don't even know of your existence there. Father gave it out to my in-laws that you had died in some accident, and told me never to talk about you. Neither my son nor my nephew knows that I ever had a black sheep of a brother."

Things were falling into their places. Anit listened with bated breath.

"Oh, before I go, do you know, I've come across Meera after all these years! She's just a house away!"

"The Meera you were friendly with at school?" asked the old man.

"Yes, and she was asking about you. How's Houdini, she asked the very first day I met her."

"Ah, she remembers that nickname friends had given me in those days! Well, well, she must have been pretty impressed with those tricks I used to show you kids," the old man sounded pleased.

Just then, there was a violent tug at Anit's shirt-collar.

"What are you about, you punk?" shouted a belligerent voice. Anit turned and looked up. Pulling at his collar was none other than the man who had attempted to rob Dadi of her bag. Vinod-the-jailbird. In a shiny shirt.

Questions and Questions

There followed a scuffle. Anit clawed at Vinod and pawed at him and bit at him. But he was no match for him. In seconds, Vinod had Anit pinioned helplessly against the wall. Anit could smell his sweat and bad breath as he hissed, "Out with it! What are you doing here? You live so far from here."

"It's none of your business what I do and where I live," cried Anit. "Besides, how do you know I live far from here?"

Before the man got his reply out, two voices came floating out of the window beside which all this was taking place.

"What's up? What's happening here?"

"Why, Anit!" Although Anit could not turn back and see, he sensed that Dadi and the man had heard the noise and come to the window.

Although Dadi was taken aback for a moment, she rallied immediately. "That's my grandson – let go of him." Anit could hear her shout and stomp out.

Meanwhile, the sleepy old man at the doorway had come up to where Vinod stood pinning Anit to the wall. "How did this one get in?" the old man asked Vinod.

"That's for you to say," retorted Vinod.

Just then there came out Dadi and the grey-haired man she had gone to see – Houdini, as Anit too began to call him. Puffing and panting, Dadi went up to Vinod and gave him a tight slap. "Hands off my grandson, you ruffian! I had let you off that day, but this time I'll have the law on you!"

"What's all this, Vinod?" asked Houdini. Obviously, he knew the jailbird!

Everybody began to speak at once, and in the general confusion, Vinod relaxed his grip. Anit saw his chance and broke away from Vinod. Run! Run! Hands balled into fists, teeth clenched, he ran. Somehow, he reached the taxi and flopped on to its thick seats.

"What's the matter?" Oh God, thought Anit, now it is the taxi-driver with his questions. He gestured him to keep quiet and wait for Dadi – who could be seen at the end of the lane – slowly making her way towards them. After a minute or two, Anit sat up. As his body relaxed, he unclasped his hands and found a bit of shiny material in his right palm. He must have torn it off Vinod's shirt. As he looked upon the shiny bit, he knew how Vinod had known where he lived. The second time they had come with Dadi, he must have seen them and followed them to the area where they lived. It must have been him who had been hanging around their house in the night, swathed in a shawl that did not quite conceal the shiny material underneath.

But then, could one believe Houdini's denial when Dadi had accused him of following her to the house? "Why did you do such a foolhardy thing yesterday?" She had asked and Houdini had laughed in reply. Coupled with the fact that he had a magician's robe (however old) of shining blue, surely that meant he was admitting that he did go over to their house. Which one of them had been there, then? Or had it been both?

Anit spoke out his questions as soon as Dadi reached the taxi and asked it to start.

But Dadi had questions for Anit as well. "How dare you spy on me?" she accused Anit. "I told you to stay in the taxi. How dare you disobey?" Trembling with rage, she flung her question at Anit. "Don't you have any respect for my grey hair?"

Anit thought it best not to answer. He knew that whatever he said would be taken as answering back.

The taxi made its way through the sparse Sunday traffic and soon crossed Mehrauli and Chhatarpur. It re-entered Gurgaon and sped through Ghitorni, Sikanderpur, Iffco and Huda City Centre. Anit saw his familiar home territory, Padam and his cart, and then the house that belonged to the Naths.

"Stop!" As the taxi reached the Naths, Anit saw his chance to get away from Dadi's wrath. "Let me get down here, Dadi. I forgot all about reading the paper out to Mr. Nath, and it is already 11."

"11.15," the taxi-driver consulted his watch.

"He waits for me to come on Sundays, Dadi," Anit made his voice full of concern. "It'll be a big disappointment for him if I don't turn up."

Dadi gave a stiff nod and signed for the taxi to stop. "Let us both get down here," she told Anit. "I feel like having a chat with Meera." To the taxi-driver, she said, "What's the fare?"

While Dadi paid the fare, Anit ran up to the gate.

It was beyond the usual time when Anit passed this way, and the sun was high up. There was no Mr. Nath sitting out with the newspaper, nor any Gaju watering the plants. The gate was latched, but unlocked, as it usually was during the day, and Anit shoved a hand in through its grille and undid its latch.

Dadi seemed to have started an argument with the taxi-driver over the fare. She was still at the corner of the pavement, talking to the driver at the same time as counting out her money.

Suddenly, there was a deafening roar and a motorcycle – arriving from the direction of the mall crashed onto the gate, throwing Anit off balance. He clutched at the gate to prevent himself from falling, but nevertheless fell hard upon the stone pavement. Picking himself up with an effort, he saw Ponytail–video camera on the back–charging into the garden through the gate that Anit had just managed to unlatch. He rode his motorcycle over the flowerbeds, dislodging some bricks from their borders, and crushing some plants in their beds. He stopped near the garden-tap, to which the hosepipe was attached. He bent down, picked up the hosepipe and turned it on to Anit, almost blinding him with the spurt of water. "*Arrey, arrey*, what are you doing!" Dadi shouted from where she stood at the edge of the pavement, but fat lot did Ponytail care.

He now moved the motorcycle forward and parked it right over the hosepipe, squeezing it flat. Stopped from flowing through the pipe, the water now spurted out at the source – where the pipe was joined to the tap. The pressure made the pipe come off, and water from the tap began to gush onto the ground.

Ponytail threw off the pipe, and laughed at Anit, all wet on that wintry day. "Feels good– isn't it! I was just passing when I saw you in a taxi –and felt like giving you a scare!" said Ponytail.

"Thank you for explaining, "Anit tried to be sarcastic.

"You here, what do you think you are doing?" cried Dadi. She had finished paying the taxi and hurried towards them as best as she could.

Ponytail gave Anit a push and he fell against the wall, hurting his elbow.

With a hoot of laughter, Ponytail re-started his motorcycle and roared off.

Water was gushing out of the tap and, flowing over the hosepipe that had got detached, spilling onto the ground. Anit turned the tap off and angrily flung the hosepipe away. It fell right under a rose-bush in the corner.

He looked around. The flowerbeds were in disarray, with tyre-marks on earth wet with water that had spurted out when stopped from flowing through the pipe.

Dadi placed her hand on Anit's shirt. "You're sopping wet!" she exclaimed. "And hurt too, I think?"

"A bit," replied Anit, which was less than the truth.

So he was actually rather relieved when Dadi said: "Let's get home now. While you change, I'll get my Ayurvedic ointment out. I must put that on your elbow. It's the second time you have been hurt today.

Yes, Vinod-the-jailbird's blows too had by now started to ache.

But what about visiting the Naths, which is why they had got off from the taxi there? As if she had guessed his question, Dadi said, "We'll come over in the afternoon after we have rested a little."

It was only when Dadi and Anit trudged up to their own front door that Anit knew what had been nagging at him for some time. All that noise, but why did Mr. Nath not open the door? Mrs. Nath not cry out in complaint? Gaju not rush out?

Darkness Falls

At lunch, there were *parathas* stuffed with cauliflowers – fresh products of the season. Golden-white cubes of *paneer* swam in rich red gravy in the casserole. In little glass bowls, there was tomato *chutney* – a specialty of Ma's.

In the midst of this wonderful lunch, there rang the telephone.

It was Chandan. "Mom's just rung up from Durgapur," he informed Anit happily. "*Nanaji's* pulled through yet another time, and Mom will be back soon."

Anit, in turn, told him all about the morning's event. He told him so in full colour and detail, winding up only when he overheard Dadi say (most loudly and distinctly), "What an unearthly amount of time children are on the phone these days!"

It was winter and the days were getting shorter. Anit went out to play within an hour of his lunch. Although Bimal and Deeksha were not there, there were others – children from their block as well as the next. Anit did not have to miss out on his match. It hurt a little, especially when he did the fielding. But oh, the wonderful feeling when his fingers closed upon a ball about to go for a six.

As they took a break, sitting side by side, and eating some early oranges, Chandan came out with the details of his *Nanaji's* paralytic attack.

"It's the right leg this time," he said. "The left jaw is all twisted up; nobody can understand what he's saying. Earlier, he could write and communicate, but now his writing has got so jumbled up that nobody can read what he's written. But Mom said his heart is still like a young man's. So said the doctors, and he may live on for years."

"You mean," said Anit, "that he's not popping off just now."

"Yes, and that's why there's no point in Mom's hanging around there."

"I wonder what Stickler is doing nowadays," said Chandan suddenly.

"I'll ask at the school tomorrow," said Anit. Chandan nodded. Someone at school would know. "How is Chhaya?" asked Anit. Chandan was silent.

Light was fading. The wind was getting chilly. They two of them stood up to go home.

"Anit, it's too terrible to get old, isn't it?" asked Chandan."And pop off?"

"Don't know, *yaar*," answered Anit, starting to walk. "But I too wonder sometimes."

Chandan wanted to go straight off to his house. But Anit made him accompany him to the Naths. Although it was growing, he did not feel like going past without looking the Naths up. He wanted to tell Mr. Nath that he would make up for today by reading to him on another day. Besides, it bothered him that no one had opened the door today, in spite of all the goings-on at the gate.

"Who's that now?" He wondered as the redbrick house came within sight. There was someone standing at the door of the house. "Oh, it's Dadi!" He exclaimed as he drew nearer.

She seemed enormously relieved to see Anit.

"I've been standing here for the past half an hour and no one has been opening the door. No one seems to be in the house. But how can that be? At least Meera would be there, wouldn't she?"

Anit looked at the house. It did seem to be silent and empty.

"Gaju! Where's Gaju?" He looked around for him, but could not see him anywhere.

He knocked loudly on the door and then began to hammer on the wood. It had a Yale lock that locked from inside, even if someone pulled the door shut from the outside. The door was clearly locked now, whether from the outside or the inside.

Evening had clearly fallen now and it grew darker by the minute. Yet there were no lights within the house, not to speak of any answers to their now frenzied calls.

"Perhaps Gaju's gone out to get milk or something – and just then Mr. Nath received some invitation to go out," Anit offered a suggestion.

"As if Mr. Nath would leave Meera like that without even waiting for that Gaju to come back!"Dadi pooh-poohed the idea.

Anit tried to think of other explanations as well. "Perhaps they have all left the place," he said at one stage, knowing all the while that he was saying something very silly.

"Don't be absurd," remarked Dadi immediately. "As if Meera could be removed so suddenly! As if she would let herself be removed! Wouldn't she want to meet me one last time?"

"Yes, of course, she would," Anit tried to calm Dadi down.

"Call your father and get him to break this door down," shouted Dadi, sitting down suddenly on the steps at the foot of the door. "My head is going round and round. I'm going to faint."

"Wait a bit, Dadi, don't faint just now!" urged Anit. "I have an idea," Chandan broke in. "Let me go round the house and see if I can –"

"No point," remarked Dadi. "I have already done that, and the back door's locked as well."

"Yes, yes, it must be," said Chandan. "But perhaps I can still –"

With Dadi sitting where she was, Anit and Chandan ran to the back. Anit almost tripped over the garden-hose below the rosebush but spared it no thought. The backyard was almost as well-kept as the garden in front. There were some empty tins and cans in one corner, and a small pile of bricks that had not been needed in the repair of the house. But otherwise, the ground had been cleaned of its weeds and cacti, and a kitchen-garden begun.

But the light was failing and anyway, Anit and Chandan had no eye for such details just now. They went right up to the back door and banged at it. There was no angry cry from within the house, as would have been natural. They banged again and again. No, there was no response.

"I know what to do," said Chandan. He dragged Anit by the hand to another door – a smaller one – that stood to the right of the back door. This was the door of the bathroom and opened in the backyard. It had a lock on it and a push showed Anit that it was securely fastened from the inside. That did not bother him. It had always been like this. What mattered was the big window atop the door. In the times before the Naths, Bimal, Chandan, and Deeksha had often made their entry into the house through that window. For, it had been without grille or glass, its original tilting window-pane being broken long ago.

But now it had a shining glass pane, which Mr. Nath must have put in when he began to live here. For a moment, Anit and Chandan stood despondent and defeated.

But then Dadi appeared round the corner of the house. Impatient to know what Anit was doing at the back, she had got up from where Anit had left her. "I told you there's no point trying from the back!" she remarked.

Without a word, Chandan picked up a brick from the pile in the backyard, and flung it up at the bathroom window. The glass pane shattered into a thousand pieces, leaving only the empty window-frame. It was – as it had been – big enough for a kid to crawl through.

"Come and stand here, Dadi," said Chandan. "Lean on the door and stand firm. We will have to get up on your shoulders."

"What nonsense!" exclaimed Dadi indignantly. "I won't allow such a thing!"

"Dadi, be a sport," said Anit, who had seen Chandan's point. "See that window? That's how I will get into the house. But to reach it, I have to raise myself up – we have to climb onto your shoulders."

"All right, but take off your shoes before you do that," Dadi gave in.

It took several attempts now. Dadi flopped down the first time, just as Anit grabbed hold of her shoulders. The second time, she fell down against the door. The third time, it was Chandan who missed. But finally, one after the other, the two were up on the sill. They squeezed themselves through the window-frame, and jumped onto the bathroom floor.

Blood On The Buddha's Head

It was even darker within, and Anit had to grope for the latch of the bathroom. He got it and then realized that the bathroom was not only latched but also locked from within – possibly as a safety precaution. The two made their way out of the bathroom. They tried the back door. That at least was not locked, only latched.

Chandan unlatched it and let Dadi in.

As he knew his way about, he led Dadi on. In the half-gloom, the house was absolutely quiet. Uncanny. For a moment Anit felt a chill down his spine. But then he felt the talisman under his shirt. Strength surged into him.

"Meera!" Dadi cried out in a quavering voice. Again and again, her cry rang out. But there was no answer.

"Oh, what a fool I'm being!" exclaimed Chandan and felt on the walls for the switchboard. He remembered roughly where it was and in a minute or two, there was light. They looked all around the room they were in. From their positions in the walls, shelves, and corner-tables, the broken statues and paintings stared back at them.

Then – at one go – they made for the room at the corner – and raised its curtains.

Dadi screamed, while Anit and Chandan stood stunned.

For, there on the bed lay the beautiful old lady, with her pillow red with blood. Anit felt his legs begin to shake, but he put his arms around Dadi, who seemed not to be able to stop screaming. He led Dadi around the bed to make her sit on the chair beside it, and then, gripping Chandan's arm, tiptoed forward.

Lying on the floor on that side of the bed – and so invisible from the door – was Mr. Nath. His head was bloody – and there was blood on the stone Buddha that used to repose on the nearby bookshelf, but now lay on the floor.

"Elderly Pair Done to Death!" – "Brutal Murder of Aged Couple!" Anit could see the headlines in the newspapers tomorrow, even as he screamed. Headlines he could never read out to Mr. Nath. Headlines Mr. Nath would never be able to listen to.

Pity, as well as horror, filled him and he screamed "Murder!"

But just then, he heard another noise. A moan. His screams stopped by themselves – just as they had begun. Body tense, he looked down at the floor. Yes, that is where the moan had come from. From the inert body that lay on the floor.

Letting go of Dadi for a moment, he sat down beside it and bent towards it. Yes, yes, he was alive, Mr. Nath! His chest was rising and falling – although so slowly that it could hardly be seen. And even as Anit listened for it, there came another sound – a long-drawn-out sigh – a painful drawing of breath. Anit looked up. The head on the pillow shifted a little.

"Dadi!" Anit jumped up, and then pulled at her from where she had sunk down, still screaming. "It's not all over yet."

Chandan sat her down on the chair and said, "Just wait here till I get help."

He knew the first thing now was to ring the police up. But the Naths had not yet got their telephone connection – he remembered Mrs. Nath complaining. So the only thing now was to go get the neighbours. No, better still, go home and tell Anit's parents and his! And, of course, ring up Bimal and Deeksha. But he had no need to do either.

Even as Chandan went out of the room, he heard the bangs on the front door, and even as he opened it, people rushed inside. A passer-by had heard their screams and come in with some neighbours along that lane. It was they who now took control of the situation.

"Police! Call the police at once!" said they. One of them brought out his cell phone and began to press its buttons.

"Call the doctor!" cried Anit. "First, the doctor!"

"No, it is the police, who must be informed first," said someone. "It is a police case!"

"Yes, the doctor cannot touch them unless the police have been here first!" agreed another.

"But that's wasting precious time!" cried Anit. "What if they are dead by the time the police come?"

"That's the law, Anit," said a familiar voice. Baba! He had also arrived, and as Anit saw this, a tremendous sense of relief surged through his veins. Baba was here!

People kept coming in. Neighbours, members of the Residents' Welfare Society. In minutes, the empty house was bursting full of people, and the police. A First Information Report was lodged against 'person or persons unknown'.

Bimal and Deeksha, who just had come home from their trips, had also rushed there.

And Gaju. At last. With a bag full of vegetables which rolled out as he dropped the bag and ran into the house. "What's happened? What's all this?" he cried at the sight of the two inert bodies with the police by their side. "O *Amma!* Who's done this to you! O *Saab,* Why have you left us like this!"

"Quiet, Gaju," Anit put out a comforting hand. "Don't cry like that. They are still breathing."

Gaju looked dully at him.

"They'll be taken to the hospital as soon as the police are through with them," said Baba.

"It's not hopeless as yet," added Anit.

Gaju's eyes began to shine and then they brimmed with tears and he burst into fresh tears.

"*Arrey,* what all this noise? Who's this?" A policeman came up grabbed hold of Gaju. Another began to ask him questions. A small crowd gathered around the distracted fellow.

Meanwhile, the doctor arrived, and also ambulances from the local hospital. "No time to be lost!" said the doctor after a quick look. "They must be moved immediately." The police and the medical men got busy. Some of the others tried to help, while some others moved away.

Anit and Chandan began to tell Bimal and Deeksha all about the events of the evening.

Suspects

Even though it was Monday, Anit had not gone to school. Ma had not let him. After the experiences of yesterday, she thought he needed a day of rest. The newspapers had not only carried news of the attempted double-murder, but accounts of the brave boys who alerted the people about it. It had mentioned their parents, their addresses and their school, with the result that the phone at Anit's place had been ringing all morning, till Baba had angrily put the receiver down.

"If you go to school," said Ma, "you'll just have to tell your story over and over again, and not get a bit of rest. You can do that tomorrow, but today, you need some rest. No school today."

Chandan rang up to say that his father felt the same.

That was fine by Anit, especially as he had a cold coming on and aches all over his body. Also, a Geography test had been fixed for today and he could think of nothing but the murder attempt on the Naths.

The Naths were now in the Intensive Care Unit of the local hospital. Neither had regained consciousness. Nobody knew how to contact their next of kin. Any kith and kin of theirs, for that matter. Whatever Dadi knew was hopelessly out-dated.

"I'll go and sit it out at the nursing home," Dadi had offered.

"I won't hear of such a thing," Baba had put his foot down.

"But how can I let Meera lie there all alone?" Dadi had protested. "You're young. You don't understand what it is like to have your childhood friend in the ICU. It's like having a part of your own self lying there."

"Nevertheless, I won't hear of it," Baba had been firm.

Ma had provided the solution. "I'll go and sit there part of the time," she had offered.

"Why, that's sweet of you, *Bahu*!" Ma had looked very pleased at that. She had then rung up Chandan's mother, who was quite a friend of hers, and worked out a time-sharing scheme with her.

That is why Dadi now lay resting in her room and Anit in his, this Monday afternoon. The wintry sun came through the window and fell on Anit's brightly covered bedstead. It made patterns of light and shade on the bedcover.

Anit too was trying to make a pattern in his head. Who tried to kill the Naths? He tried to figure out. Who wanted to kill them and why? The police had questioned him and Dadi yesterday. They had asked again and again about how they came to break into the house and discover the misdeeds. They had asked Dadi about the incident. They had also questioned Gaju narrowly.

"What do I know about all this?" Gaju had whimpered. "I watered the garden as usual and then *Saab* asked me to go get vegetables for tomorrow. He himself closed the front door when I left. It was then 4 o'clock. I know because *Saab* told me that and said that I must be back by five."

"*Bachhu*, you weren't back by five, were you?" One of the policemen had remarked. "You came in much later, at quarter-past six. So everyone here says."

"*Sach*, Sir ji. And that shows I wasn't even in when all this happened."

"We shall see," the policeman had remarked. He had aimed a sudden blow at Gaju's head and Gaju had cowered back. "Don't hit me, Sir. I haven't done anything."

"We'll find out," the policeman had said. "Know about finger-print tests, idiot? You will see what we do to you if we find your finger-prints on that statue."

"But of course you are going to find my finger-prints on it. I dusted it, I handled it, so my finger-prints are going to be there in any case." And Gaju had begun to sniffle.

Baba had protested against browbeating and bullying Gaju just because he had been a servant in that household. "Instead," he had remarked, "why don't you check if anything valuable is missing from the household? Even as a layman, I can see that this house is full of valuable antiques." He had succeeded in diverting the policemen's attention. They had let go off Gaju for the moment and gone off to check the house for evidence of a burglary.

Gaju had clung to Baba's feet. "*Saab*, don't let them take me to the police station! They'll beat me up and make me say anything they want to."

Dadi too had pleaded with Baba. "He's a good boy – I have seen him obey every order of my friend's with a smile – and my friend had become quite difficult these days. She was an invalid, as I told you, and, in any case, she had been a bit of a spoilt child even in her childhood. Hard to please. Always asking for attention. But this boy put up with all her tantrums."

Baba had seen to it that Gaju was not taken into police custody, but allowed him to spend that night in the house itself. After all, the Naths were not dead, and might live to require various things from home to be brought to the hospital.

Gaju was the main suspect. In the eyes of the police; it was he who was guilty. But was the case as simple as that? Anit had his own ideas about the case.

The nasty fellow on the motorcycle – it could have been him at the bottom of it. Hadn't he come in that very same morning, making a nuisance of himself? But then he had left in the presence of Dadi and Anit, and without any scene with the Naths. No, it could not be him. Well, why not, Anit thought again. He could have come back after they were gone. He could have caused further damage to the garden, and this time Mr. Nath could have been provoked into making some protest. No, even that was all wrong. Mr. Nath would not have invited him into the house to break his head up. He would have settled the matter outside. But then perhaps he was doing so, and Mrs. Nath had heard the voices and called out – just as she had done when Anit had come there the first time. Perhaps he had come in and was shutting the door, when Ponytail had barged in after him, and followed him to where Mrs. Nath lay. Perhaps there had been a big scene afterwards. And then the brutal attacks. Afterwards, he could have taken a round of the house, and pulled the front door shut after him. Yes, but when could this have had happened? According to Gaju, everything had been fine till 4 o'clock, when he had been sent out shopping. Besides, if it had been him, wouldn't he have tried to make away with something of value? The small portable television set, the music system, or the antiques? There were also the steel almirahs that could have at least been tried.

Nevertheless, Anit had told the police about Ponytail this morning and the police was trying to track him down. Ma and Baba had told them about the fellow in the shawl who had been loitering near their house. Perhaps he had really been watching the Nath residence from there. It seemed that one or two other neighbourhood families had also noticed him, but not given the matter due importance.

Anit had a further problem which he was dying to discuss with Bimal, Chandan and Deeksha, and Dadi too – because it involved her in a big way. Anit had a hunch that it had been jailbird Vinod who had been loitering there under cover of darkness. If not on both days, at least on one. He had been wearing a shirt of shiny blue stuff yesterday, which might have been the very thing that had shown under the loiterer's shawl. He felt sure that Vinod had followed Dadi and himself to their neighbourhood. Somehow, he knew that Dadi had some valuables with her. He also wanted to get even with Anit and his friends for not letting him rob her of them the very first day he had tried. He should – he must–tell the police about Vinod. But how could he do so without telling them about Dadi's secret trips? About her rendezvous with mystery-man Houdini? Brother though he may be to her?

Bimal and Deeksha were at school. So Anit had to wait before he could have them come over for a discussion. Before going out, Baba and Ma had been very clear that he should just rest all day at home. He waited impatiently for the afternoon.

The doorbell rang.

Anit went out to the little balcony outside, and looked down. He could not see who it was, but rushed down hoping it was Dadi. He peeped through the 'magic eye' of the door and stood stock still for a moment. Then he pulled his shirt-collar straight, and opened the door —- to let Stickler in.

No lesser a personality than Stickler!

Sorting Things Out

"Good Morning, St- I mean, Sir, please, Sir, sit down." Leaving the door open, Anit hurriedly indicated one of the chairs in the sitting room. Why had Stickler landed up here? How did he know where to come? Or had he come just by chance?

Stickler stood as usual, steady and erect, hands on the well-known stick. His hair, Anit took in at a glance, had more grey in it. Otherwise, he looked just the same. Wait, no, at the moment, he had deep lines on his forehead.

"The police visited my house earlier this morning, at 11 A.M., to be precise," Stickler said grimly, "in connection with the attempted murders you discovered yesterday."

Anit felt so stunned at this that he clutched weakly at a chair for support.

"I, Sir, well, I,"he stuttered.

"You, Sir, did the correct thing," and Stickler sat down. "I thank you for it."

There was another bell and this time *was* Dadi. "Dadi, this is – was – I'm sorry – our Principal, Mr. Pradhan." Stickler immediately stood up again and folded his hands in a *Namaste*. Dadi returned it and came forward. After a few more words of introduction, the two of them sat down, and Anit went to the kitchen and brought water to drink as he had been taught to do every time someone dropped in.

"To go back to the purpose of this visit," began Stickler, while Anit stood at attention as if in the Assembly. "I believe

Anit here has reported my son to have entered the premises of the household concerned, and even caused some damages to the grounds. I believe, madam, that you have corroborated him. I also believe that both of you have spoken the truth."

Anit swallowed hard. "Your son! But that was Ponytail!"

"Jaydeep does indeed sport one," Stickler said coldly.

Jaydeep!

No, it cannot be. It was inconceivable. But it turned out that Ponytail was indeed Stickler's son and named Jaydeep Pradhan.

"A spoilt brat. Totally out of control."

"But, Sir," Anit found the words bursting out from his throat, "you have been so strict with us – kept a whole school under control."

"I know, I know," replied Stickler, hitting the floor with his stick. "I've succeeded with two whole generations of students – not to speak of the staff – but I have failed with my own son." He kept his head down upon his two hands – hands that gripped the stick so hard that the knuckles stood out white.

"What about your wife – his mother?" Dadi asked.

"He lost her long ago and perhaps I have never been able to make up for that loss."

"Ah, I see," remarked Dadi.

"I was scared of spoiling him," Stickler went on, "and tried to discipline him in every way. I did not want people to laugh at me and say, 'Ah, there he is, swinging his stick at everyone's child but his own. And in consequence, I possibly became too strict with him. So strict that he broke away from my control altogether."

"Where does he put up?" asked Dadi. "Doesn't he stay with you?"

"In the same brick-and-mortar structure, yes. But we hardly see each other."

"Doesn't he have a job?"

"Freelance journalist, at least that's what he says. Always on his motorcycle. Always with his video camera."

Anit began to understand and he felt a great pity for both the father and the son. It is so difficult to judge people, he thought.

Stickler suddenly raised his head and looked Dadi in the face. "But however out of hand he's got, my son is incapable of violence of this sort! Hitting the old and the invalid – no, I'm sure he couldn't have done it."

I'm not so sure, thought Anit, remembering the incident of Padam and his puppy. Should he tell Stickler about it? But somehow, when he looked at his lined forehead, he could not add to his burdens. Instead, he said, "Sir, let's go over the whole day once more. Perhaps something will strike us. Perhaps we can figure things out better."

And so Dadi and Anit started all over again.

Stickler listened with full attention, his eyes narrowed. He made Dadi and Anit go over certain points again and again. "Hmmmph," he remarked from time to time. After a while, Dadi went to the kitchen to make some tea. Anit went on with his story.

Suddenly, shadows fell across the room through the open doorway and Chandan called out in a cheery voice, "Look whom I have brought over!" He gave a start as he saw who was within,

Anit too gave a start. He had not realized it was about 4 o'clock, the time by which he and his friends normally returned from school. What startled him more was that beside Chandan stood........

A spectacled man in crumpled clothes.

Who came in even before Anit had had the presence of mind to welcome him?

Who almost tripped over Stickler's stick and emitted a loud "Oops!"

Who then warmly clasped Anit's hand and said, "I'm so proud to have you in my school!"

The new Principal. Mr. Neogi whom the school had, by now, nicknamed 'Neo'.

It was a bit mind-boggling, thought Anit, having not one but two Principals in the house, suddenly. But he pulled himself together and did a round of introductions.

Neo seemed awestruck at meeting Stickler. "It's a great honour, Sir, to meet you. I've been meaning to go over, Sir, and ask you for your advice in running the school. I don't seem to be able to do much with it. In fact, I don't seem to be doing anything at all with it."

Stickler gazed at him icily. There was clear disapproval in his eyes. But Neo seemed to be utterly oblivious. "Bit of good luck, the double-murder, I mean. Well, not quite murder but murderous alright. It was only because of that, that I came to see Anit; it was only because I came to see Anit that I met you. Yes, it's a bit of good luck."

"Not so for the couple concerned," said Stickler. "Nor for those suspects."

"Guess not, Sir," said Neo, happily. "But talking of suspects, who are they? Tell us about them, Anit! I love mysteries and here's one in our very midst!"

Dadi came in with the tea, and after she had been introduced to Neo, and he to her, Anit began his story once again.

A Process of Elimination

"Leave nothing out," added Stickler every now and then. "Something that seems insignificant can be of vital importance."

So Anit mentioned every single detail he could remember. However, he left out Dadi's secret trips to Arjun Nagar, and all Chandan's nudges could not make him say a word on the matter.

It was dark when Anit stopped. Full twenty-four hours had passed since the discovery of the gruesome attempt, and evening had fallen once again.

As Anit stopped, the phone rang. It was Ma from the hospital. There had been no improvement in the condition of the Naths, and she was now so tired that she was coming home. Dadi got up and went into the kitchen to get something ready for her.

Baba rang almost immediately afterwards. He was on his way home from the office. "Well, I'll push off now," said Neo. "Sorry, I haven't been able to have any bright thoughts, but perhaps I'll have some in the night. Be sure to come to school tomorrow, Anit, so that I can share them with you."

He turned to Stickler and said, "Are you too pushing off, Sir? No? Well, I had thought we could have a chat on the way – about the school, you know, Sir. But, I guess it will have to wait. Anyway, it was great good luck on my part – meeting you here, I mean, Sir, not the murders – I mean the assaults," he added hastily, on seeing Stickler's expression.

Chandan too went off with him.

Stickler and Anit were alone now, with Dadi pottering about in the kitchen.

There was a strange silence between them, and then Stickler said, in a voice that Anit had never heard from him, "My poor motherless child, Anit, I'm sure he's innocent. He may have been *around*, I admit, but he's never been *in*."

"But who could it have been, Sir? What do you think?"

Stickler shrugged and got up to go. Then he paused at the doorway. "What about that man-servant the newspapers mentioned?" he asked.

Walking him to the gate, Anit said, "No, Gaju wouldn't do a thing like that."

Why should he and how could he? Would he then be watering plants and buying vegetables instead of running away?

Ma, when she returned, explained that the Naths were not yet out of danger. She was too tired to say much more. Even Dadi did not press her. Instead, she passed a hand over Ma's hair and asked her to go to bed as quickly as she could. "God bless you for being kind to us old people," Anit heard her say softly.

Baba, when he returned, said that he had met Gaju on his way. Gaju was going to the hospital. He would spend the night outside the ICU, he said, till someone took over from him in the morning.

A Long Night Descends

That was a long night. Anit had rested himself so thoroughly during the day that he lay wide-awake, listening to the intermittent sound of the night watchman's stick upon the pavement somewhere in the distance.

He probably had a cold coming on, thanks to the dousing Ponytail had given him. A cold wind was blowing through a window that had not been closed properly. Anit got up to close it, and chanced to look out.

What was that? Anit froze. A man swathed in something dark – possibly a shawl – atop their gate. Even as Anit watched, the man clambered over the gate with great difficulty and landed on this side with the slightest of thuds. He stood for a second with his hand on his chest, as if this effort had tired him out. In that second, Anit caught the flash of blue and silver again beneath his shawl. Was it Houdini then? Or Vinod-the-jailbird?

The figure began to move – to tiptoe towards the house. He stopped before a window downstairs – one just below Anit's own – Dadi's. He peered in through the glass and then tapped gently.

Where was the night watchman? Anit could find him nowhere in sight. He knew he should move fast and wake everyone up – warn them – help them catch the man – ring up the police – inform the Residents' Welfare Society – and so on. But he found his legs would not obey him.

And in those petrified moments, he heard the window open, and Dadi hiss out, "Here again?"

"Don't shout, Champa – don't wake people up – I haven't come to ask for more money."

So it was Houdini.

"Why have you come at all?" Dadi said in a helpless way. "What will I do now?"

"I have come to tell you something important –"

"Some new trouble, it must be, that you have fallen into," Dadi interrupted him bitterly.

"No, no, Champa. It's something about this attempted murder or robbery that the papers reported today. I read the papers and felt I must come to you."

"Impossible! That is what you are. If you have been involved in that terrible thing, it is the last thing you should do – come here and risk getting caught."

"But I have nothing to do with that!" the man exclaimed.

"Softly," cautioned Dadi. "What is it then? If it is not –"

"That's what I have come to tell you, but you are not letting me!"

"I'm just scared that is all – what's going to happen if my nephew finds out about you – if –"

Anit did not wait to listen any more, but crept out of his room. No, it would only waste time to wake Baba and Ma up, and perhaps give Houdini a chance to escape. No, he would first catch him, and then raise the alarm. Silently, he went down the stairs, to the front door. Opening it with the smallest of clicks, he went out, crept behind the dark figure, and encircled it with his arms.

"Baba! Ma!" Anit began to shout, as Dadi gave a wail of despair.

Houdini tried to break out, but Anit realized that he was an old man, and gave up within seconds. He stood limply within Anit's arms, and panted heavily, with his hand on his chest. Within seconds, Baba was there, taking Anit's captive into his own control. Ma too had run out and behind her, there was Dadi.

"Get back in and dial 100," said Baba to Ma and began to pull the hapless Houdini in. "Wait, listen to me," Dadi was trying to tell Baba as she followed him into the house.

A window opened in the house next door. "Any problem there?" Their next-door-neighbour's voice came floating.

"No, Uncle," shouted Anit before Baba could answer.

"But we heard something!"

"Mew!" said Anit loudly. "Just a cat, Uncle, bothering us," he then shouted out. It was a cold night and the neighbour drew back and closed his window.

Anit rushed back to the house after the others.

Baba was holding Houdini fast, while Ma had picked up the phone. Dadi had sunk down upon the sofa, her face in her hands.

"Don't, Ma," cried Anit. "Don't call the police – this is Dadi's own brother. What's more, he is the one who gave me the *kavacha* of Karna."

Then there was silence, except for Houdini's amused "*He He He He*!"

Houdini Introduces Himself

After a while, everybody began to speak out all at once. Then everyone fell silent and Houdini took over.

"Believe it or not, I am the elder brother of this venerable old lady – this picture of respectability. I, the homeless vagabond, the luckless failure. You do not know me. When my father married his daughter into your family, he gave it out that his son had died in some accident. That is the lie his dutiful daughter – my loving little sister – kept up. And why, you will ask. Because, I did not want to look after the family business. Or, join the Civil Services. Take up Law or Medicine. I wanted to be a magician – like the great Houdini. I had picked up some magic – from local artistes and books. I used to amuse my sister and her friends with my tricks. At our own home, or at theirs, and sometimes even on the roadside. I performed for them, and they loved it. They nicknamed me Houdini. But that was not enough for me. I wanted to go abroad – and train under the great magicians of Europe and America – I wanted to make a name for myself – I wanted to be famous – I wanted to conquer the world. My father could not stomach the thought. Not only did he refuse me money to go abroad, he publicly whipped me, and my mother stood watching helplessly. So I ran away, and I did so with my mother's jewellery. I sold them and got my passage money. I went abroad. But I had no luck. You see me now, an old, broken man. With massive debts to pay. I had borrowed heavily to put up my last show abroad – a big flop, sadly enough for me. Then I had borrowed heavily to buy my ticket back to India. Here, I had fallen into worse and worse times, and run into fresh debts. I travelled here and there, but I could not hire halls to hold my shows or afford any advertisements. As I became older, I tried to have road-shows and even became a peddler of magic trinkets —- which is how I met this kid," he pointed at Anit.

Ma, Baba and Dadi gaped.

"It was not a trinket," shouted Anit. "It worked. It made me brave. It brought me friends. I still wear it!"

"Ah, good to know that I did work some magic after all!" said Houdini and continued. "Well, nothing much worked and I began to pawn and sell off my equipments. One by one ... they all went. All, except this robe which I simply cannot part with. And my magic wand. My equipment was all foreign, made abroad, but the money I got was not enough for my debts. And I do not want to die with my debts unpaid. That is why I traced my sister – my only surviving relative – to Patna – where she lived with her son. My parents had died soon after her marriage and there was no one left in our old house in Assam. Well, I found Champa's address and wrote to her from here – Delhi, where I was putting up in a cheap lodging-house – along with people who were down-and-out like me. She answered – I'll grant her that – she answered at once. She even said she would help. But she would not let me go and see her in Patna. She would come to Delhi, where she was in the habit of coming every year, and here too she would not let me go and see her. Instead, she would come to my lodging-house, and bring the money with her – in various doses."

"And that's why," Dadi spoke at last, "I used to go out by myself and pass on money to my brother. Every time I went, he mentioned a fresh debt and I had to take one more trip. I used to worry about how to raise all that money. I even sold some of my jewellery – all in secrecy."

"That's what I found suspicious," added Anit. "This secrecy of Dadi's – this worry. I told Bimal and the others and they said Dadi could be dying of cancer and trying to keep it secret from us. That's when we started following her."

Baba and Ma sat listening, as though they had lost the power to speak. Baba's hold on Houdini had relaxed, and Ma had kept the receiver down.

Anit told them how he – along with Bimal, Chandan and Deeksha – had shadowed Dadi, and eventually come upon her secret. He also told them about the two encounters with Vinod-the-jailbird in his shiny blue shirt.

"All this was going on and you didn't even tell us!" Ma sounded hurt when she found her voice.

"If you had once told me!" said Baba, looking reproachfully at Dadi. "I would have taken care of everything. I wouldn't have let you worry so much – go through such a lot."

"I was scared," Dadi confessed, "that I would come down in your eyes if you learnt I had a brother like this! Besides, father had made me promise never to mention him to anyone in the family I married into."

Baba looked hurt. "You have forgotten," he said, "that I loved magic shows – well, when I was small."

"But aren't you going to let me say why I am here tonight?" Houdini broke in. "I didn't come here to rob or kill, you know. Neither tonight nor that other night when this kid saw me."

"Of course not," said Baba soothingly. "But – er – why did you come?"

"That's what I was trying to tell Champa when the kid grabbed me from the back. Anyway, I had come that night to find out where Champa was staying. I watched the house for a while, saw her face at a window, which I guessed must belong to the room she was using. And then suddenly, this little chap caught sight of me and raised the alarm. I had to move off. Of course, my purpose had been served. I had found out how to get in touch with Champa, instead of waiting for her to get in touch with me. It came in useful today – when I came to tell you about Vinod,"

"Yes, yes, tell us about him," Anit urged.

"Vinod is a rotten fellow – like me. Never made any good.

Even went to jail a number of times. He hung about the area, and knew many of its inmates. He came to know me, and would often ask me to show him a trick or two. Honestly, I quite liked that! And so I began to open up to him, and he to me. I must have mentioned why my sister came to me and he must have guessed that she carried her money in that bag of hers. The temptation must have been too much, and when she was going away, he must have made a snatch at the bag. Yes. That I do see. But what I *don't* see is Vinod doing those murders – which hopefully will turn out to be just attempted ones. I remember Meera when she was a schoolgirl in Guwahati. She liked my magic tricks then. I would have loved to show her a few more now."

Dadi put her *pallu* to her eyes at this.

Baba was however relentless. "With all due respect, well -er -Uncle," he said, "why can't that jail-bird have made those murder attempts? He did have a shiny blue shirt and he did follow Anit to this area. The second time Anit saw the man – that's when I was also there – he ran away, actually ran away. Now that I think of it, it could not have been you there. You couldn't have run like that. It was the run of a young man."

"Right, right, that's what you are," agreed Houdini. "It was me the first time, when this kid was coming down the lane and saw me. But the second time, when all of you saw someone from this place, it was Vinod. I know because he told me about it. He reported the whole thing to me because *He-he* ! It was I who had guided him here."

"And why was that?" asked Baba, with a return of coldness in his voice.

"I knew your house – I had found it out with the help of the address I had got out of Champa. But I did not know the exact house where the Naths lived. I told Vinod to come here, then observe the whole area, and find out."

"But why?" everyone asked in one voice.

"As soon as I tell you that, you will realize that Vinod – rotter and bounder though he is – could not have killed the Naths. He just wanted to see them – to catch a glimpse of them – no more."

Everyone stared.

"I know that feeling," Houdini went on, "I have also been a son disowned."

"You mean – that – that horrible man – that jail-bird – is Meera's son!" Dadi cried out in shock and disbelief.

"Yes, I told you that we used to chat sometimes. In course of those conversations, I realised that he was the son of a girl who was my sister's friend, a girl I had known once. A link with my young, innocent past! I felt a strange affection for him. He had told me his history then, in bits and pieces. I knew he had been a juvenile delinquent – thrown into remand homes – but never reformed. His parents had grown so ashamed of him that after a while, they had refused to take him in. Refused even to see him. That had forced him to go back to crime – petty pilfering, chain-snatching and the sort. Homeless, he moved from place to place, losing all touch with his hometown or his relations. He went to prison so many times that he came to be called Vinod the jail-bird."

"How long has he been flitting in and out of–Tihar jail perhaps?" asked Baba.

"Well, he has been in Delhi and its outskirts for three or four years at least. But he had no idea that his parents too had recently moved to Delhi. He got to know that only by chance when he followed this kid and his friends here–the second time they went to Arjun Nagar with Champa. He had not been able to snatch Champa's bag that day, and wanted to know where she lived, so that he could waylay her again. And then he caught a glimpse of Mr. Nath – his father."

"What did they say to each other?" Dadi bent forward with eagerness.

"Nothing – they never spoke. Vinod said he turned and ran."

"Why? Why didn't he go up and say who he was?" Anit asked.

"Because he did not have the gall to face his father. Because he knew his father would not let him in. He had disowned Vinod completely, didn't I tell you?"

"Yes, that's right," thought Anit. He remembered that the Naths had not kept anything in the house that reminded them they had a son – not even a photograph. He had found it odd even then. People with children settled abroad usually kept their photographs all over the place. . Nath's boast that he had two sons and four grandsons ; Mrs. Nath's calling for the photo album to be shown to Dadi; Narendar and Birendar, settled in Boston and Dublin; the golden-haired daughters-in-law .... all that had been cooked up to cover for a son the parents did not want to call their own. The album that could not be found was just not there!

But there was another question that puzzled him. "Why did he come back in the night?" Anit asked.

"He hankered for a glimpse of his mother. He went back again and again, in the evenings. He walked up and down the street, stood in dark corners, and watched out for his mother to take a walk in the garden, or at least come to the balcony or window. You see, he had no idea that she was a bed-ridden invalid now. He learnt that only today from the papers, just like I did."

"Why, didn't I mention it to you that day?" asked Dadi.

"No," replied Houdini. "Maybe you meant to, but couldn't. Vinod had grabbed hold of this kid just then – and we had rushed out."

"Well," said Dadi, "I'm glad that Meera's son has some feelings for his mother."

"And that is what I came to tell you," continued Houdini. "He hadn't become such a hardened criminal as to have no human emotions left. To have tried to finish off his own parents." He paused and went on. "You see, I read in the papers that this boy stated he saw a suspicious character around – I knew if the police questioned him further, he would sooner or later talk about his adventures in Arjun Nagar and his encounters with Vinod. With Vinod's prison records, it would be easy to trace him out. And once they found his father's name in the records, it would be easy to trace him to this crime. He's a criminal all right, but not guilty in this case."

"But then who *is*?" Anit suddenly found himself shouting.

"Someone's bashed their heads in. It can't be Ponytail because he is Stickler's son. It can't be Houdini because he's Dadi's brother. It can't be Jailbird Vinod because he is the Naths' own son. Who can it be then?"

He walked away to a window and impatiently drew the curtain aside.

"It's getting to be morning!" He exclaimed the next moment.

They had not realized it, but hours had gone by, and the eastern sky was no longer dark. As it began to grow lighter by the second, Dadi began to chant as she had done all the other mornings:

Jabakusumasamkasham –

"Ah, the chant father taught us in our childhood! You remember it and so do I! Our common inheritance!" Houdini suddenly turned upon Anit, "Well, what about your chanting the same? You still have Karna's *kavacha* with you, don't you? When I peddled that to you, I had no idea that I was doing it to my grand-nephew!"

Next Morning

Anit woke up groggy. His throat felt sore. But he did not want to miss school two days in a row.

With everyone tired and sleepy after talking through the night, he got ready a little late and had to run to the bus stop, his water-bottle swinging.

"Where are you off to?" asked Chandan, Bimal and Deeksha, coming after him. They were laughing and none of them had school uniforms on. What was more, there was Chhaya with Chandan today! And she came up to Anit and began to dance with him. It felt good, though it ruined his shirtfront. But why were they all out like this?

Yesterday it had been declared that it would be a holiday today. The school cricket team had won in a State tournament.

"We are off to the park," said Deeksha. "Come along!"

Anit wondered if he should first go home and take off his school uniform. As he had told Chandan, he looked after his own uniform. He did not want it crushed unnecessarily, and dirtied more than Chhaya had already dirtied it. But it seemed such a waste of time – especially with this extra holiday.

Padam came by, pushing his cartload of vegetables, Pappu prancing about around the wheels.

Padam stopped when he saw Anit, and asked if he knew whether the Naths were better. Then he shook his head and remarked, "I guess those juicy cabbages will just go rotten now – and all those other vegetables I had sold Nath *Saab* the very same morning. What else, with the two of them lying in hospital! And such fresh ones they had been that morning, those cabbages!"

Chhaya meanwhile had been rubbing noses with Pappu, and even ran after Pappu a little when Padam pushed off. She did not seem to be exactly in the shadow of death just now.

"Better, isn't she?" Anit asked Chandan, who nodded.

"She is old, there's no denying that. But those pills Sharma Uncle gave the last time? They seem to have worked," said he.

"Good, *yaar*," answered Anit. "It's not all over for her yet. She still has life in her old bones. Like Stickler, like Dadi, like Houdini, like Padam." They all looked at Padam in the distance.

Bimal giggled. "Padam seems more concerned about vegetables than about people!"

Anit and Chandan also smiled, but there was a frown on Deeksha's forehead. Something in Padam's words seems to be bothering her, thought Anit.

But before he could ask what it was, Anit saw Sanjay, Tarini, Ranjit and a few other senior boys coming towards him. It being a holiday, they had thought of looking Anit up and getting first-hand-accounts of the crime that had made headlines. So they all sat down in the park, making a ring, and Anit told his story once again. He even told them about Stickler's visit to his house last evening, followed by that of Neo. He did not leave out the night's events either. Sanjay and Tarini asked Anit question after question, their eyes shining with excitement.

Ranjit, however, kept quiet. When Sanjay and Tarini had finished with their questions, he said slowly, "I feel so bad about Stickler now. He's not had an easy life – with his wife dying and his son getting out of hand. But he's still done his best for the school."

"I know," agreed Anit, "Done more for us than for his own son."

"I wish I hadn't played that nasty trick at his farewell, *yaar*," said Ranjit. "He must feel he has failed both with his son and with his school. Every time he looks at that silver stick, that's what he must think."

Just then, they saw Neo was hurrying along the road, possibly to Anit's house. He was dressed in sleeping *pajamas* and clad in bathroom slippers, but did not seem to remember that at all.

Anit got up and ran to him, followed by others.

"I was going over to your house, Anit. Good that I found you here. Oh, you're dressed for school, are you! I am sorry I forgot to tell you that I had declared a *chhutti* today. I had done it myself but – well with the excitement of the murder, I mean, assault, I absolutely forgot. Well, now, Anit, I had said I might have some bright ideas by morning. Listen to this. If those fellows on the motorcycle had created such a racket outside around lunchtime, and nobody had even come to the door or shouted at them, then there's just one explanation. Gaju was not in and the Naths had already been done in – almost so, I mean. And that," he continued, "fixes the time of the crime at lunch-time rather than four in the evening as we have been taking it to be."

"But Gaju says he went out only at four and the Naths were quite okay then," commented Anit.

"So it wasn't a bright idea after all!" Neo looked crestfallen.

Anit saw Bimal and Chandan smile. But Deeksha looked very serious. "Why did Mr. Nath send Gaju out for vegetables in the afternoon," she asked, "when he had already got them from Padam in the morning?"

"*Arrey*, you are right," said Bimal wonderingly.

"Padam mentioned a little while ago," Deeksha continued, "that he had sold some great juicy cabbages and things to Mr. Nath that day. So Mr. Nath already had a stock of vegetables at home. Why should he then send Gaju out for vegetables again? That is what has been bothering me ever since we spoke to Padam."

"Yes, why did Mr. Nath send Gaju out at four?" repeated Chandan.

"Could he have done it to send Gaju out of the way?" asked Neo slowly. "So that he could smash his wife's head in? And then bash his own head to avoid suspicion?"

All-round silence and then Anit, sore throat forgotten,

shouted out, "NO!"

"People have done such things before," said Neo. "I have read it in so many Agatha Christie murder mysteries – I adore them, you know, I have got all 80 of them. Well, Agatha Christie said that whenever a wife is murdered, it is usually the husband who does her in."

Before he could go on, Anit cried out "No" again. "No," he cried, "Mr. Nath wouldn't have done such a thing. He loved his wife. He loved his wife so much that he would not leave her side to get his own eyes operated. He wouldn't take the risk of getting blinded, he said. He would rather let go of the chance of seeing better. That is why he used to ask me over to read the papers out to him, and that is how I know he could not have killed his wife."

"Cool down, kid," said Ranjit, who along with Sanjay and Tarini, was leaning on the park railings.

But Anit would not cool down. "There's another reason," he cried, "why he wouldn't have done such an unfair thing as killing an old, invalid lady on her bed – no, even if she was not his wife. He was an umpire, and he was always for fair play."

"Yes," agreed Bimal, "He had umpired a game of ours as well, and he had been fair to all of us."

Just that instant, something else stuck Anit.

All Along It Was...?

"Gaju had been watering the plants BEFORE he went out to get the vegetables. But then why should the hosepipe have been lying under the rosebush when we went there in the evening? He would have coiled it up and put it away. But I remember it was there still – I almost tripped over it as I ran to the back of the house."

"Are you sure?" asked Chandan, while others stared.

"I am," said Anit.

"Then there's just this – Gaju must have been lying," declared Chandan.

"And why should he have been," said Bimal wonderingly, "unless – unless he's got to do something with the affair."

"He may also have been lying over the vegetables," added Deeksha. "We don't know for sure that it WAS Mr.Nath who sent him out to get them. It's just that he is saying so."

"We have only his word for it that he saw Mr. Nath alive at four," continued Anit slowly. "And, yes, there had not been a sound from inside when Ponytail had made such a racket outside. I had found it odd even then, but I was wet and hurting all over and I went home and then forgot all about it."

"So you see," said Neo, "the murder attempt may very well have taken place before lunch-time, and it could very well have been this Gaju."

"But, just supposing it is, why didn't he run away afterwards?" asked Deeksha. "Why did he come back with that lie about the vegetables?"

"He possibly knew that he could not run far enough. He had, I think, already had some trouble with the police. He had an idea about how the police – how fast they were, and how they worked," said Anit. "I remember him pleading with Baba not to let the police take him away and make him confess."

"So he must have done something like this to throw off the scent," said Neo. "Gone out soon afterwards and maybe seen a movie or something to kill the time – or simply hung around the place. Got some vegetables from the market, and kept watch on the house from a distance. He may have seen Anit's brush with the fellow on the motorcycle, or he may not. What is more or less likely is that when he saw that the crime had been discovered and everyone was crowding there, he came in himself, pretending to have gone out at four."

"So clever!" exclaimed Bimal.

"So cunning!" agreed Chandan.

"So cold-blooded!" remarked Deeksha.

Anit was too horror-struck to say anything.

It was Sanjay who now spoke. "But what motive could this Gaju possibly have had? Especially as he had not made off with anything? "

Ranjit echoed him. "Yes, what could have made the fellow do such a thing?"

"That is bothering me too," added Tarini.

"Where is Gaju now?" Anit asked slowly. "Ma said he would be at the hospital until someone took over from him in the morning."

"Then he may have come back by this time," said Chandan, beginning to run towards the redbrick house of the Naths. Chhaya scampered after him, and in a minute everyone else followed.

The police had put their own lock on the gate, and sealed the front door. But who cared for all that? One by one, they vaulted over the low garden wall – and ran to the back of the house where Gaju's little shed stood. Neo reached faster than some of the others! Chhaya began to bark, seeing that something exciting was about to happen.

"Gaju!" called Anit. Others began to pound on the door of the shed. Some went to the sides and the back.

"Give yourself up, Gaju!" hollered Anit. "The shed is surrounded on every side!"

"If you try to run, we will set the dog on you!" yelled Chandan.

The door was opened.

Gaju stood there, eyes half-closed. One look at all of them, and he collapsed on the ground. "Don't let the police arrest me!" he whimpered. His eyes were those of a hunted animal.

The others were in favour of ringing up the police immediately, but Anit wanted to get Baba there first. He also wanted Dadi by his side. "Don't let him escape, guard him, all of you, while I bring Baba and Dadi over." With that, he rushed home.

He found that Ma had gone to the hospital again, in spite of the sleepless night she had spent. Houdini was fast asleep on the sitting-room sofa, and Dadi was in the kitchen making Baba a late breakfast. Hurrying them out of the house, quickly explaining on the way what had happened, he returned. Baba kept up with him, taking long strides. Dadi came huffing and puffing and crying, "Wait!"

Deeksha and Tarini had tied Gaju to the door of the shed with the *dupattas* of their *salwar-kameez* suits. Everyone stood in a semi-circle around Gaju, who still sat on the ground just outside the shed.

Dadi came up and stood before him, arms akimbo. "Before anyone says a word, I have something to say. Annu, your mother rung up from the hospital a little while ago. The Naths are out of danger and although they are still in the ICU, they have both regained their consciousness."

"God has answered my prayers," exclaimed Gaju and raised his *dupatta*-bound hands towards the sky. In the mid-day sun, the relief in his face was clear to everyone.

"Tell me how it happened," ordered Dadi. "Meera's said a few things, but she can't speak much, according to *Bahu*. Nor can her husband. So I want the story from *you*."

"I hadn't wanted to hit *Amma* – I really hadn't. But she scolded so much – she was scolding me all the time. I did all she asked me to do, but I had never a soft word. It was always, Gaju, have you gone deaf – or, Gaju, you idiot – Nothing that I did was right, nothing that I did was enough. That day, it was the tea that was too cold, the soup that was too hot, – till I could not bear it. I don't know myself what happened. I was watering the plants but she kept on calling me! I had to leave it and bring her this and that, and, when I had done all those chores, to dust the bookshelf in her room– right then. Forgetting about finishing my task of watering the plants, I had to start dusting. I had just picked up that statue thing to dust, when she started off again. Gaju, *tu mar gaya kya* (Are you dead that you cannot hear me), and I suddenly brought the statue down upon her head. *Saab* was there – right beside her on the chair, and he caught at me. I was scared, it was nothing else, believe me, I was scared that he would call the police and I hit at him with the same thing – God forgive me."

While the others struggled with their speech, Dadi shot out, "What did you do next?"

"I sat shaking with fear, sat and wondered what to do. I heard someone calling outside – then there came the noise of a motorbike and some people shouting – it seemed from very near the front door. But I kept quiet. I didn't even get up and see what it was. I sat like that for at least an hour. Then I went out through the front door. You know how those doors lock if you pull them shut."

"Well, afterwards?"

"I hung around – I went to Iffco Chowk and bought a bus ticket to Alwar, but I didn't feel like going after all. I don't remember exactly what I did – I just remember being worried and miserable. I knew the police would suspect me. And they would suspect me all the more if I tried to run away. And in any case, where would I run away? Jaipur? Alwar? I have no home to run away to. Before I came here, I have lived on railway platforms and under flyovers. I have even been in prison before. I tried to think of a way I could avoid suspicion. I bought some vegetables. I stayed near the crowd in the mall, coming up from time to time, to see if people had discovered what I had done. When I saw that they had, I came in and you know what I said and did after that."

"Yes, Gaju," said Anit, "you acted very well then, crying for *Amma* and pretending you knew nothing about what had happened. Your staying up outside the ICU – that must have been acting too. Well, it had really taken us all in! It made us believe everything you said!"

"It wasn't all acting," Gaju began to cry. "I wasn't acting when I was crying for *Amma*. I wasn't pretending when I was sitting at the hospital." He beat his *dupatta*-bound hands on his head. "I never wanted to hit *Amma* or *Saab*! I hated myself from the moment I did it!"

"Oh yeah?" asked Ranjit. "Was that why you left them there for hours, bleeding away? If you had at least got a doctor, or tried to do something for them, I would have believed you were feeling bad about what you had done."

"You don't understand," wept Gaju. "I didn't think I *could* do anything for them – or a doctor either. I didn't think there could be things done for them. They lay there so soundless and still – I thought I had killed them – absolutely finished them off. And when I cried for *Amma*, it was not acting. I was crying from relief, crying because they weren't dead after all – at least not yet."

"Hmphh," said Dadi, very loudly. "Perhaps you are not all bad – but I do wish Champa had not taken in someone without checking the past."

Baba agreed. "Clearly, the fellow's been in trouble with the police – no one knows what violent streaks there may be in him. If the Naths had gone in for police verification or at least tried to find out about his antecedents, none of this may have happened."

"But," said Gaju, "*Saab* knew about my police record."

"Why had he taken you in then?" asked Baba, astonished.

"Yes, why?" echoed Dadi.

"I had never wanted to do all that, picking pockets and snatching purses. But on the streets, they make you. The *dadas*, the *goondas,* they force you. If I went to prison, it was only because of them. When I came out this time, I decided I would not go back to them. I would become a gardener, or a servant, or anything that would give me a roof over my head. I tried here, I tried there, and finally, Nath Sa*ab* took me in."

"In spite of knowing your history?" Baba still seemed unbelieving.

"Well, *Saab* used to say that he had a son whom he had thrown out because he had turned out to be a rotter even when he was at school. He had come once or twice for shelter, but *Saab* had been so angry and ashamed of him that he had not taken him in. Well, *Saab* too had been young in those days. Now he was old and felt bad about being so tough on his son. He wondered where he was – and said that he would give me the chance he had not given his son – sort of trying to make up to God, I felt."

"I see," said Dadi. "Yes, I am beginning to see."

So was Anit. He saw it another way. Mr. Nath collected broken things. Gaju was also a broken thing. He looked all around and asked, "What do you think we should do with him?"

"Hand him over to the police!" came some angry voices.

"Don't be too harsh with him – let him be!" came some softer ones.

Everyone stood there for a while, debating and discussing what they should do about the murderer who was not a murderer after all.

Finally it was Dadi who spoke.

"My heart is full of happiness today – my friend and her husband are not going to die – I don't have to lie and cover up about my brother any more – and if you knew what a relief that is! Well, today I don't find it in my heart to give this wretched creature up to the police." She cleared her throat and went on, "Let's wait and see what my friend and her husband have to say. Let the police carry on by themselves. Let Gaju stay here. If he runs away, we'll alert the police."

"I won't run away," cried Gaju, "I'll stay on at least till I've fallen at *Amma's* feet and asked her to forgive me. Then if they throw me out or hand me over to the police, I'll feel less bad."

"That's settled then," said Dadi briskly. "Untie him and come home, all of you. I'll fry you some hot *pakodas* before you go off home."

"Can I come too?" There was a whisper in Anit's ear.

"Of course, Sir," said Anit to Mr. Neogi. "You are one of us now."

Next Sunday

Anit quickened his pace as he drew near the redbrick house of the Naths. Dadi had already gone there, along with her brother, that is, Houdini. It was Sunday and Anit had a cricket match to play in the park. But before that, he had to visit the Naths who had come back from the hospital late last evening. His parents and Chandan's had brought them back. The newspapers had carried reports of the case for a couple of days. But as it had become clear that the elderly couple in question was not going to succumb to their injuries, papers had dropped the matter. In the neighbourhood, in the Residents' Welfare Society, and sadly for Anit and Chandan, in the school, interest in the matter was dying down.

He came up to the gate of the house.

Gaju was there in the garden, watering the plants with the hose. The old grin was back on his face as he let Anit in through the gate.

"*Amma's* taken me in," he said as he took Anit inside. "When they brought her here from hospital, and put her down on the bed, I just fell upon her feet. I cried and cried and asked her to forgive me. I would not let go of her feet and in the end, she got cross and asked me to go make some soup for her."

As Anit moved the curtains aside and entered, strips of coloured paper came floating around him. Why, they were coming from Houdini's shirt-sleeves as he sat on a chair by Mrs. Nath's bedside! "*He He He*," he laughed, "I was showing Meera some magic."

"As in the old days," said Mrs. Nath in a faint voice.

Yes, Mrs. Nath it was. Anit could not take his eyes off her. Thinner than ever, with a bandage around her head still, she looked as beautiful as ever, with the silver hair spread over a pillow that mercifully was not blood-stained like last time.

Mr. Nath too was there, but on a bed this time. The bookshelf (along with the Buddha) had been removed, Anit noticed, and a folding cot brought in and fitted into the room. On it lay Mr. Nath, a bandage on his head as well. He held out his hand and Anit went up to him.

But before he could say anything, someone else came into the room. "Baba, shall I then –" He stopped short on seeing Anit, and there was a very awkward moment. Then Vinod-the-jailbird came up and gave a (rather forceful) pat on Anit's shoulder.

Dadi too had come in and she explained the situation to Anit. "They have come together, you see, father and son."

"It was she–your Dadi – who brought that about," said Mrs. Nath. "Yesterday, when we were about to be released, Champa told us all about Vinod, and – that man," she pointed at Mr. Nath, "headed straight for that Lodge or whatever Vinod stays in. He hugged him and wept, as he told me, and came back with him. After keeping us apart all these years with his strictness and so on. After torturing me, in fact."

"It's not that I did not suffer," muttered Mr. Nath.

But Mrs. Nath went on. "It was that really which had made me so bitter, not my legs. I know I was hard upon everyone – and Gaju got the worst of it. I can understand his nerves snapping that day –"

"Are you sure, Meera, that it is a good idea to take Gaju in after all this? Won't you feel scared to have him hovering around you?"

"No, I know it was my fault. I had driven him to it. He was at the end of his tether and he just – lost it."

"It's gone out of him, that pent-up feeling," explained Mr. Nath. "I too feel like giving him a second chance."

"If Vinod can have one, why not Gaju? He too calls me '*Amma*', doesn't he?"

"You were always such a sweet girl," said Dadi huskily. "But don't talk so much now, Meera, or you will get tired. I want you fully rested and recovered before I go next week."

Yes, Dadi was going back to Patna next week, to see if her son, Uncle Samit, could work out something for her brother there. For the time being, he would remain where he is, and then join her at Patna. "Little Annu" knew that he would miss Dadi, especially after the exciting times they had gone through together this time. But he knew that Houdini would make up for her absence, as he had promised to come over every other day to teach Anit, Bimal, Chandan and Deeksha some of his magic tricks. Neo had dropped in just when this was being discussed, and expressed a strong interest in attending Houdini's classes. But he had told Anit sadly afterwards that Stickler had got in touch with him and persuaded him to go in for lessons with Stickler on the Principles of Education.

Meanwhile, Mrs. Nath was trying to get Mr. Nath go for an eye operation, of course, when he was better.

"Meera's right," said Dadi, "and with Vinod by your side you need not worry about what will happen to Meera if the operation fails."

"Yes, that is right," agreed Mr. Nath. "I'll definitely consider going in for a cataract operation as soon as I can. But in the mean time – Anit, here is today's paper." With hands that still trembled, he pulled out the newspaper that someone, possibly Gaju, had placed below his pillow.

For once, Anit was glad to do so. Soon Bimal, Chandan and Deeksha dropped in to see the Naths. They all took turns at reading out to Mr. Nath.

"*Kahan mar gaya, Gaju*!" Mrs Nath called out, smilingly. "Bring out *laddus* for all of them!"

"*Hanji, Amma ji*," and Gaju was back with the *laddus* and his old, familiar grin.

Houdini's Incredible Tale

Houdini began to drop in very frequently at Anit's place. "Why don't you move in with us?" Baba and Ma often said to him. But he refused every time. "What have I got, except for my own, independent way of life? Let that much remain with me." But he came often, all the way from Arjun Nagar, with his vast repertoire of magic tricks and incredible yarns. Every time he came, Anit rung up Bimal, Chandan and Deeksha, and together they sat around Houdini, having a great time. They learnt quite a few card tricks and the art of blowing out paper streamers at will. They learnt to make handkerchiefs change colour and pots shoot out paper plants. They also heard about Houdini's travel adventures.

"Come on, don't pester him so," Ma said one such evening as she brought in home-made *kaju barfis* for him.

"It is a long time since I had home-made food, and sweetmeat at that," Houdini sounded a little sad. "And *Bahu*- may I call you that as the long-lost brother of an aunt of your husband? (Ma nodded with a smile)Well, *Bahu*, I don't mind telling the kids about my wanderings. What are their names? Anit, Bimal, Chandan and Deeksha – quite the ABCD gang!"

They all liked that, and ABCD became their name.

"What should *we* call you?" asked Chandan. "Of course, you are a Dadaji to Anit. Shall we all call you that?"

"Well, what do you refer to me as, among yourselves?"

"Houdini," Bimal answered like a shot.

"Uff," said Anit. What if 'Houdini' took offence?

For a moment, he just looked at them. Then he burst into laughter. "*He He He He*! I like that! Houdini!! Meera, my sister's friend, Mrs. Nath now–used to call me that. I like it. It's a compliment. Houdini! Please continue to call me that, ABCD."

Then he went on to tell them about his adventures.

He had returned by the sea and with only a rucksack upon his back containing his equipments and accessories for magic. He had hardly any money. So he took a bus from Bombay to Goa where he had a friend named Alvarez. He ran a school there in a village by the Cavelossim beach in South Goa.

Shaded with trees, creepers and ferns, the village also had a water-body or lake that had long ago been connected to the Arabian Sea. It was now marshy at the edges, but deep at the centre. It stood silent and empty, the year-round. Only some ducks took dips in it, and a few herons and cranes picked out food along its fringes. But it came to life in the winter when migratory ducks and teals flew in and made the waters a sheet of quivering, quacking and flapping grey and white.

All day the ducks stayed on the water, fishing and floating. Then, just before sunset, they rose to the sky in great swirls, and flew away to some paddy fields in the distance.

In the morning they were back again. This went on for the whole of winter. At the beginning of summer, the birds went away. Along skyways of their own, to Siberia, Canada and other such far-away lands.

"I loved to see them rise and fly away," recalled Houdini. He began going to the lake almost every evening. Some villagers also came there to see the ducks and Houdini would show them some magic and earn a few rupees.

But mostly Houdini was by himself. One evening as he sat there waiting for the ducks to take wings, he saw a man come up the muddy bank. Houdini had not seen him before. He was bearded and had unkempt hair. He wore a tired-looking suit of clothes and carried a big, black bag with him. He placed it on the bank, opened it, and took something out of it.

Houdini happened to be sitting behind a clump of reeds, and the man did not see him. Houdini could watch him, though. He saw the man go down to the edge of the lake and catch hold of a duck. It tried to get away, but the man held it fast between his thighs. In his hands, he was holding something sparkling and he brought it down upon the duck.

Why, it was an injection syringe.

Released, the duck waddled into the waters and was lost among the other ducks.

Houdini went up to the man and asked, "Hey, what was that? What were you doing to that duck?"

The man quickly put his syringe away into his bag and began to ask questions rather than answer them. Was he from this village or an outsider? How long would he be here? And so on.

Houdini too kept asking: "Where are you from? And who are you? And what were you injecting that duck for?"

"I am Dr. Bhide from Pune," said the man. "I am an ornithologist. I study birds, especially migratory birds and their routes."

"But why did you give an injection to that duck?" asked Houdini.

"That was a dye I injected into it," answered the man. "It will colour its feathers yellow and I will be able to recognize it more easily. I want to see if it comes back here next year as well. Like Salim Ali putting rings round the feet of birds in at Bharatpur Lake in Rajasthan."

"I see," said Houdini. "But I hope you have the government's permission to do what you did."

Without any answer, Dr. Bhide hurried away with his bag.

The flapping of a thousand wings filled Houdini's ears. The ducks rose from the lake, and the glowing sky was all dark for some minutes. Then as the ducks flew away, flock after flock, the lake was empty and silent again.

Alvarez had a friend named Captain Roderiques who liked to hunt and sometimes even took a few shots at the ducks. Once he had come over to Alvarez's place and the conversation had turned to the ducks in the lake. "This time their number seems to be coming down fast," Captain Roderiques had said. "When they came they had covered the whole lake. Now they don't even cover half of it."

"But how is that possible?" Alvarez had scoffed. "Unless it is you who is shooting them down!"

"I have nothing to do with it!" Captain Roderiques was indignant.

"Come now, Captain Roderiques," said Alvarez. "Only a few days ago you had asked us over for a meal of roasted duck!"

"Well, er —-" grumbled Captain Roderiques. "I may have gunned down one or two of those silly creatures. But certainly no more. But now there are at least a hundred ducks less."

"Perhaps they are being shot down by poachers from the next village," suggested Houdini.

"No. Then we would have heard the reports of the shots," said the captain.

But if it was not any poacher, who was killing all those ducks?

That is what Houdini was wondering that evening, as he gazed upon the sheet of water before him.

Suddenly, in the gathering gloom, a huge snake-like neck shot up from the water.

The ducks close by scattered and took to their wings.

Houdini stood up with excitement.

But what was it? No snake could hold its neck so stiffly. Was it a swan then? But no swan could have such a long neck. Besides, swans were white and this one was grey. And it had a small, flat head atop, more like that of a huge lizard.

Then, before his eyes, the neck dipped down and swiped at

a duck. Houdini could see it struggling within the jaws of the creature. Just for a second. For, it dipped down again, and was lost in the darkening waters.

Houdini rushed to the village with his news.

"You are making it up," said Alvarez and a few others like Captain Roderiques.

Village lads gave up taking dips in the lake or playing on its banks. The lake lay still and deserted.

As a friend, Alvarez asked Houdini not to go there. What if some unknown danger was lurking in its depths? But Houdini did not quite give up his visits to the lake.

A few days later, as he sat there among some reeds watching the ducks and teals in the gathering twilight, he caught sight of the same Dr. Bhide who had injected a duck with a dye.

The man was just going forward into the lake.

"Stop, Dr. Bhide," Houdini warned him. "Don't go further. It's risky."

The man started and whipped around. He had probably not noticed Houdini earlier among the reeds.

"Risky? Why so? Why?" he asked.

"Some strange creature has got into it. It's eating up all the ducks!" replied Houdini.

"What!" The man's tone was full of delight.

Puzzled, Houdini explained the whole thing to him. He was shocked to see Dr. Bhide look more and more pleased as he went on.

As Houdini finished, Dr. Bhide clasped his hands together and said, "Success at last! My years of work have at last become successful!"

"What!"

Before the man could answer, there was turmoil in the waters.

"Look! There it is, rearing its head!" shouted Houdini.

The sheet of ducks was torn apart from the surface of the

lake as the long black neck emerged. It stayed there for a while, swaying high above the ducks.

Dr. Bhide went into a silent rapture.

The neck swooped down. The jaws at the end of it opened wide. They caught up a duck, chewed at it, then splash! The neck went under again.

"See? It's a huge snake eating up the ducks," said Houdini.

"It is nothing of the sort. It is no snake at all," Dr. Bhide's reply came pat.

"But we both saw it!" exclaimed Houdini.

"What we saw was the neck of a Plesiosaur," said Dr. Bhide.

Anit and his friends looked at one another. They were aware that 225 million years ago, the earth had contained, not men, animals, birds and fishes as we know them, but gigantic creatures called dinosaurs. The Ankylosaurus, the Brachiosaurus, the Protoceratops, and the Tyrannosaurus were dinosaurs which moved on land while the Plesiosaur was a sea-creature. It had flippers rather than legs and a very long neck. Its head was small and flat and the long jaws were full of sharp teeth. But around 65 million years ago, either the coming of the Ice Age or the crashing of a meteorite- no one is sure what–made dinosaurs suddenly go extinct. They became fossils embedded in the earth while a whole range of other creatures came gradually to life: animals, birds, fishes and, of course, humans. So the creature in the lake of them just could not be a Plesiosaur.

"Impossible! Absurd!"said the ABCD.

"I too had said the same to that Bhide," Houdini said. "It is Bluff. It is Bullshit."

"It is not bluff or bullshit," Bhide had answered, "but my handiwork, my achievement." He had gone on to explain that while some of the dinosaurs had died out, some had changed themselves slowly into the lizards and birds of our times. A garden lizard is a form of the old gigantic creatures, and so is a bird. What Dr. Bhide said he had tried to do, was to take the modern bird back to its original form. To make birds, which have evolved from dinosaurs, become dinosaurs again. The injection he had given the duck that day was no dye. It was a serum that he had made. It would change the functioning of certain glands and hormones, and take the duck as close as possible to the Plesiosaur family.

"Why did you choose this lake here?" Houdini had asked Bhide.

"Because the Plesiosaur was a marine creature, and this is a sea-water lake. My creation; it would be in its natural habitat of saline water. It would have an ample diet of ducks, and not get torn to pieces by sharks before I brought it to the notice of the world."

"But that's not fair," Houdini had said. "Why, think of the poor ducks! One can't use them like this. Like – like fodder."

"Oh, what do a few ducks matter! Look at what I have created! Look at what it means for science!"

The neck came out again and grabbed one more duck. There was a flurry of feathers and a dying screech.

One part of Houdini had been aghast while the other part had marvelled at this fantastic show of magic – as he saw it. Re-creating an extinct creature! Bringing a dinosaur back to life! Could it even be possible! Then he had come back to reality and got up to go.

Dr. Bhide had caught him by the shoulder. "Where are you going off to?"

"To the village. I'll tell everybody there about this, and they will kill or capture the monster and save those poor ducks."

"You think I am going to let you go? Let you ruin everything? Allow a pack of villagers to destroy my life's work?" Bhide had exclaimed. "I have developed another serum to take care of that." With lightning speed, he had brought out another syringe from his bag and plunged it into Houdini's thigh.

Houdini had fallen on the wet ground. He had felt a strange tingling sensation and then complete numbness. He had opened his mouth to scream, but could not. The injection had paralyzed

some crucial nerves of his. As he had lain there, Dr. Bhide had gone forward almost into the lake. It was dusk by then. The sky in the west was red, streaked with some grey from gathering thunderclouds.

A bird rose from the water and took to its wings. Another, then another. Soon small swarms rose here and there from the surface of the lake. A whirring of wings filled the air. Finally, the whole flock was up, moving away.

Suddenly a huge body had heaved up from the waters. Till now Houdini had only seen the neck and the head of the so-called Plesiosaur. Now he saw its entire body. It was a massive lump of grey and white, like the body of a huge turtle without its shell. There were four flippers and a rather heavy tail. The Plesiosaur began to swim towards the edge of the lake, and Dr. Bhide took out a camera from his bag and focussed it on the Plesiosaur.

It wriggled out of the lake and lumbered over the wet bank. Its flippers made it a slow walker on land.

Dr. Bhide clicked his camera. There was a flash. The Plesiosaur stopped, sniffed at the air and made a move to disappear into the waters.

Dr. Bhide went on clicking his camera.

"Hello! Are you here?" began a voice from beyond, and ended in an awestruck:"*Santa Maria*, what's all this?" Arching his stiff neck with difficulty, Houdini saw that it was his friend Alvarez, come there in search of him. His eyes were on the Plesiosaur, and so he did not realize that Houdini could neither move nor speak.

Dr. Bhide turned round and rushed at Alvarez.

"Run!" Houdini tried to tell Alvarez but could get no sound out. He saw Dr. Bhide catch hold of Alvarez and try to thrust his syringe into Alvarez as well. But Alvarez kicked and threw Dr. Bhide off-balance. Together they rolled in the mud.

Meanwhile, the Plesiosaur began to advance again.

"Aaaaagh." There was a sudden cry.

Alvarez stood up. Dr. Bhide didn't. He struggled to be up on his feet, but lay shuffling in the mud. He opened his mouth, but the scream was a silent one.

Houdini understood. While rolling on the mud, syringe in hand, it was himself – instead of Alvarez – that Dr. Bhide had pricked.

Alvarez came up to Houdini and tried to lift him and carry him on his back. But Houdini too was no featherweight and Alvarez could not. "I'll get the others from the village," said Alvarez and rushed off.

Shuffle, shuffle – the Plesiosaur had come pretty close to Houdini by now. It came even closer – and Houdini desperately tried to move. He realised that all the magic he had picked up so far was useless against this creature. Could the real Houdini too have escaped from this situation?

He looked up and saw the long neck and toothy jaws. He closed his eyes.

A shot rang out from behind. The Plesiosaur raised its wounded neck skywards and screeched. Another shot. It was Captain Roderiques to the rescue.

Voices from behind. People around him, hauling him up and carrying him back.

Houdini opened his eyes. All around him were the villagers, along with Alvarez and Captain Roderiques. The grand creature before them had crumpled down in a heap, its neck torn to pieces by the shots. Everyone looked at it in wonder. Houdini reported what Bhide had said. For, the man himself was not to be found. In the pandemonium, he had dragged his half-paralysed body somewhere into the thick vegetation surrounding the lake.

In a few hours' time, reporters and government officers landed up on the banks of the lake. The carcass was taken away to Bombay for analysis by scientists. Houdini was interviewed by newspapers. Bhide, they never could trace. In a few days, the autopsy report from Bombay arrived. It was surely an abnormal, deformed creature. But was it more than a duck injected with growth hormones? Nobody could say. Gradually, the interest in it died down. The pool was quiet again, with only the whirring of the wings of ducks and teals as they rose from the still waters.

It took some days for the effect of the injection on his nerves to wear off. Then Houdini left without a word to anyone, even Alvarez. He had the money that the local papers had paid him for his interview. And his rucksack.

Another of Houdini's Tales?

"Where did you go to? What did you do next?" Anit pressed Houdini on his next visit. Bimal, Chandan and Deeksha too were there, sitting round Houdini. Today they were in the mood for stories rather than new magic.

"After my encounter with the Plesiosaur, I had an encounter with Garuda – well almost," said Houdini. "*He He He He*." By then he had moved off to another part of Goa where there was an old Portuguese fort atop a rocky cliff rising steeply from the sea-beach.

Painfully, as his muscles were still hurting, he had climbed on to the ramparts of the fort. There were a couple of old canons lying around. Wild grass grew in between the rocks that the fort was made of. There was also an old church within.

Down below foamed the sea with ships moving in the distance. A few local people were coming up, and Houdini fell to chatting with them.

One of them mentioned a shrine he had just visited. It was very close, right on the rock-face below. Foot-prints of the bird-god Garuda had recently been discovered there and its priest had been blessed by Garuda with healing powers. "Well, why not try to pick up some healing power from him," Houdini had thought. "That is magic as well."

He had gone down the cliff to a ledge of rocks jutting out

to the beach further below. There were indeed two huge prints embedded on the rock there–three-toed prints like those of a bird or lizard, but gigantic. A cement platform or *vedi* had been raised next to it. It was anointed with sandalwood and vermilion and decked with flowers, coconuts and burnt-out incense-sticks. A red-clad priest was sitting there in a posture of yoga. Houdini had fallen at his feet and asked him to heal his damaged nerves.

The priest–Swami Garudananda – had told him about Garuda, the deity of the shrine and the king of the birds.

Sage Kashyapa had two wives, Kadru and Vinata, both of whom were very keen to have sons. The sage blessed them with not quite human sons but eggs to be hatched. Kadru had many small eggs whereas Vinata had just two huge ones. Kadru's eggs hatched easily enough and into black snakes. But Vinata found her eggs taking too long to hatch. In her envy of co-wife Kadru, she impatiently broke up one of her eggs. What came out was a half-formed bird, to be known as Arun – the red glow that ushers the morning sun in. Well, Vinata was more patient after that and let the other egg hatch in its own sweet time. After hundreds of years, it hatched into a half-bird, half-human creature. It had a golden body with red wings and legs with talons. Its face was white and its eyes were those of a bird. It became the dreaded enemy of its co-brothers, the snakes, and the devoted *vahana* or vehicle of the godhead Vishnu.

Houdini had asked the priest about the footprints. How long have they been here? Garudananda had replied that it had been there always – right from the era when Garuda had stopped here on some errand of Vishnu's. But it had been discovered only recently when a huge wave had smashed against the coast and dislodged some rocks. As the rocks had rolled away, they had revealed these marks. The same night, in his Mumbai home, the priest had had a dream or vision. Vishnu in his glorious form was commanding him to come here and guard the place, prevent the public from coming and walking all over his devoted Garuda's footprints.

Houdini had observed that the priest sat there day and night and did not encourage too many devotees to come and crowd round the place. Anyway, it was a difficult climb down from the fort which itself was a remote spot for tourists. But he did allow some villagers from another end to come regularly with offerings of rice, fruit and milk. He chanted *mantra*s over them and sold them *kavacha*s.

"I hung around him for a few days and tried to get a few *mantra*s out of him. The one to Garuda went like this:

Om Garudaya namah
Om Khagaya namah
Om Raktapakshaya namah
Om Suvarnakayaya namah
Om Vishnu-rathaya namah

Bows to Garuda, the sky-going, red-winged, golden-bodied vehicle of Vishnu. See, I still remember it," said Houdini.

But as for magical healing powers, the priest did not seem to have anything much to impart to Houdini. In fact, Houdini sensed that the priest did not really want him around. Neither did he let the other visitors go too close to the platform or the footprints. He took their offerings himself and laid them on the platform. Then he took the people away and began performing his healing rituals.

That made Houdini curious. He tried to get closer to the platform and the footprints. One day when the Swamiji had moved off for brushing his teeth and cleaning himself, he drew closer to them.

He looked at the two footprints in the pockmarked red-black rock. He tried to imagine a huge bird half-divine, standing just there, towering over the rocks lying around. It was a tremendous feeling.

"*Namah Garudaya*," he said and bent reverently towards the platform. His eyes fell upon a handle on top, cleverly entwined with garlands of flowers. So the platform could be lifted like a lid! Was there a sewer below? He then saw a torch right next to the handle, hidden under a big heap of flowers. So this was the cover of something underground, some place dark and secret!

By then Swami Garudananda had come back and Houdini pretended as though nothing had happened. He realised that the priest was clearly a charlatan, practising some sort of hoax. It would be stupid to tell him what he had found, perhaps even dangerous. But that night he just pretended to go to sleep at Swamiji's feet, keeping himself fully alert.

Past midnight, he sensed Swamiji getting up, prodding Houdini to check that he was sleeping. Then he opened his eyes a little and saw Swamiji creep quietly to the platform. He picked up the torch from under the garland and cleared the platform of all its flowers, coconuts and incense-sticks. Then pulling at its handle, he yanked the platform open like a trap-door, and kept it ajar. Switching on the torch, he stepped into the opening.

Houdini jumped up, took up his rucksack and after an interval of five minutes or so, also stepped into the opening.

"Didn't you fall and hurt yourself?" asked Chandan.

"No," answered Houdini "I found that there were rough-hewn steps into the cavity that had opened up. Was it leading to the basement of the Portuguese fort above? I could see Swamiji ahead of me. The torch in his hand lit up the way for me. He had not yet sensed that I was following him. And then the passage widened and I saw that there were electric bulbs on the walls. On the uneven floor that sloped down under my feet, I saw something white. Why, it was thermocol! There was also bubble-wrap lying around. Why, there were several cartons neatly piled up. Cartons of what? Portuguese gold?"

Houdini had then heard conversation. Swamiji had obviously met someone who had come along from the other end.

"Tonight another consignment will be shipped. But you at your end also need to know and take care. No one must get to know from above. Remember the reason why you have been posted there."

Houdini realised that the whole affair of Garuda's footprints was concocted stuff. A cover-up, but of what? He could sense Swamiji coming back, groping upwards slowly. He was bound to come upon Houdini. What if he hit Houdini on the head with his torch? Or even strangled him? Houdini looked around and saw another passage. It was narrower and darker but he just took it.

"Who's there?" He heard the 'someone' call out.

He heard Swamiji reply: "No one, Sir. With me as the guard, who would it be?"

The passage that Houdini had taken went past a cavern of sorts serving as a basement. He saw men engaged in packing some objects in bubble-wrap and thermocol sheets and putting them into cardboard cartons. They were doing their job with care and did not notice him stealthily creep past. Obviously, there was some smuggling going on here. Well, Goa was notorious for such activities and Houdini did not bother to see what it was that they were packing as shipment. He just thought of how to save his life. If any of these workers saw him, he was done for!

Then suddenly his passage opened into a wider, much wider cavern. Although he had no knowledge of Geology, he knew that there was a hardened bed of lava below him. Half-buried in that were bones of gigantic size and curious shape – femur bones, humerus bones, ribs, skulls and teeth. How could bones be so huge? Did they belong to some giant? Houdini was terrified. Then it struck him that they were dinosaur remains of prehistoric times. The Age of Dinosaurs, he remembered, is said to have ended with a meteor striking the earth in what is now the Deccan. Volcanic eruptions might have made dead and dying dinosaurs flow out here with molten lava pockmarked by rain. The lava had hardened in time and the remains had become fossilized. Now someone had chanced upon this cavern with its treasure-trove of ancient fossils. A geologist? An archaeologist? Instead of declaring it to the government, or to any scientific organization of the world, that someone was smuggling it out of the country for museums and laboratories abroad. Packing them in bubble-wrap and thermocol and getting big prices for them. The Portuguese had unknowingly linked their basement to these caverns. The smuggler–or perhaps a whole gang–had made use of it, to pack and store their consignments. They could have sealed up the tunnel leading up and above. But what they had done was to keep it intact as a secret passage of escape. Only, they had needed to post a guard above to prevent anyone from knowing about their operations. Swami Garudananda was that guard and he had cleverly made use of a rock with dinosaur footprints, and his stories about Vishnu and Garuda.

"All this flashed through my brain but honestly my only thought then was to get out as quickly as I could out of this underground maze. So I just moved on, forgetting my strained muscles, and muttering, don't ask me why, "*Garudaya namah.*" And then, I suddenly came upon a break in the wall of the cavern."

Houdini had scraped out through it, rucksack and all. Where he had emerged was probably the other end of the rock formation above which the old Portuguese fort had been built. For, the sea could be heard but not seen.

It was still dark but he had found his way to the nearest bus station and got out of Goa.

"You never tried to report the smuggling to the police? Bust that racket?" asked Baba who had also come in some time ago and been listening to Houdini's account.

"I was just too glad to be out alive," confessed Houdini. "*He He He He.*"

Yet Another Yarn?

"I say, Houdini is good at spinning his stories," said Chandan at school the next day.

"Stories? You mean he was just making fools of us?" said Bimal.

"*Aur nahin to kya*?" laughed Chandan. "Plesiosaur from the past! A cavern full of dinosaur fossils! Huh! Impossible!"

"Were there any dinosaurs in India at all? Dino fossils seem to be found only in Mongolia or America!" commented Deeksha.

"Of course not!" came a response from Madam Paramjeet who had overheard their conversation in the school corridor.

She told them that at one stage, India had been teeming with dinosaurs. A huge fossil had been discovered in Telengana in 1961 and named Barapasaurus Tagorei.

"Bara Pa, of course, meant 'big leg' but why Tagorei?" asked Anit.

"Because it was discovered in 1961 and that was the birth centenary of Rabindranath Tagore," answered Madam Paramjeet.

60 feet tall, 13 feet wide and weighing about 20 tonnes, the Barapasaurus had proved that dinosaurs had existed in India in the Jurassic period. A left femur from it had been brought and displayed at the Museum Of Natural History in Barakhamba Road, Delhi, while the rest had been stored in the Geological Study Unit museum inside the Indian Statistical Institute on Barrackpore Trunk Road, Kolkata.

Madam Paramjeet had herself seen the femur bone in a glass

case of the Museum of Natural History, before the museum had been destroyed in a fire in 2016. It had created in her an interest in Palaeontology and eventually, she planned to give up teaching and go in for research in the subject. "But what is Palaeontology, Ma'am?" Anit asked.

"Palaeo is a prefix that means ancient, Ontology means the study of the essence of beings," said Paramjeet. "It boils down to the study of fossils and dinosaur bones and other such extinct organisms. Now hurry back to the class."

In the recess, they caught hold of Madam Paramjeet again. "Ma'am, we have a doubt, no, not about the stuff we study, but..." Anit faltered.

Chandan was direct.

"Ma'am, can dinosaurs ever be brought back to life?"

Paramjeet laughed. "Well, I am sure you have seen Spielberg's films if not read Michael Crichton's books!"

"I have seen Jurassic Park 1, Jurassic Park 2 as well as Jurassic Park 3," said Chandan with dignity. "But they are just films."

"If you want to see dinosaurs in action, visit exhibitions like the one I saw last year in the USA," said Paramjeet. On a visit to her brother there, she had visited the Stone Mountain in Atlanta, Georgia. It was then holding an exhibition of animated dinosaurs. There had been dinosaurs of all kinds as if in their natural habitat. Stegosauruses that moved their tails and Brachiosaurases that arched their necks, Tyrannosauruses that roared and Pterodactyls that flew – all on mechanical and electronic power. In India too, some years ago, she had visited 'Dinosaurs Alive' at National Science Centre, Pragati Maidan. It had been a show organised by the National Council of Science. Teams of scientists, engineers and technicians had constructed robotic dinosaurs that were life-size and life-like. Models had been manufactured and equipped with pneumatic or compressed air-cylinders. "It was impressive, but completely a matter of science and technology," she told her students. "Don't waste your time on absurd issues like whether they can be restored to life..."

Then something else seemed to strike her. "Well, I do know of someone who says it is possible – dinosaurs can again come to life – but then he is regarded as a mad man."

Anit, Bimal, Chandan and Deeksha – the ABCD– at once pressed her to say more. Madam Paramjeet seemed sorry that she had mentioned the man, but in the end, she had to give in.

"Well, he is a most famous professor, but also considered most eccentric. Scientific circles have completely rejected him."

"But why?" asked Anit.

"Because of what he had once said."

"What did he say?" asked Bimal.

"Well, he said he could re-activate fossilized dinosaur eggs."

."And," Chandan asked, "Could he really do that?"

"He hardly had a chance to do so," said Paramjeet. "At the Palaeontology Congress where he made his claim, his paper was torn to pieces by other scientists. He was booed at, and dubbed mad."

"Couldn't he find anyone to get him an egg to experiment upon?"asked Deeksha.

"Well, perfectly preserved dinosaur eggs are a little different from guinea-pigs or rabbits to experiment upon. They are a bit rarer," commented Paramjeet. "And, in any case, who would try to get them for a mad man – as they thought the professor to be."

"But the man should get some chance to prove his claims," remarked Anit, with force. "Yes," chorused the others.

"If you feel like that, why don't you look him up in person?" said Madam Paramjeet. "His name is Professor Chakladar and I have heard that he lives somewhere around Gurgaon itself. If you like, I can find out exactly where, and take you along."

Her eyes were shining like a little girl's.

"Thank you Ma'am," cried her students. "That way we will at least get to hear what he says."

"Then I will ask Jaydeep Pradhan – a journalist I know."

It turned out that Stickler's son Ponytail was a childhood acquaintance of Paramjeet's. She knew that he was a bit wild but also that he had recently turned over a new leaf and trying in all sincerity, to find openings in local dailies."He's just the person!" she said. "I'll call him."

"Can you get hold of his number?" Anit was a bit dazed.

"I have it saved in my cell phone," Paramjeet said. "We sometimes go out together."

The ABCD looked at one another.

In a day they got the required address.

To Bhondsi

On the very next Sunday, the four of them accompanied their teacher to Bhondsi, which is where Professor Chakladar stayed. Instead of taking a taxi, Paramjeet drove her own second-hand car. They took the Rajesh Pilot Road and turned left at Hansram Chowk. Then they proceeded along Main Sohna Road towards Badshapur. There had been an old fort there, which had once been the residence of a queen of the Mughal Badshah Bahadur Shah Zafar. But it had fallen into ruins and become a mound where several new houses had come up. The Main Sohna Road had *dhaba*s and small shops on either side– of fruits, vegetables, grocery and stationery, *desi tambaku*, coal, cement, auto parts and so on. There were a couple of clinics and diagnostic centres. Beyond walls old and new, green fields could be seen. Here and there men were smoking decorative metal hookahs. There were small *mandir*s, *gumbad*s and *haveli*s. Nayagaon went by. There came signboards pointing left towards Bhondsi Central Jail and Damdama Lake and pointing straight towards Faridabad.

They reached Bhondsi on Sohna Road. On the left, there was the Bhondsi Police Station. On the right, the Aravali range could be seen as blue-grey waves in the distance. There were houses, big and small, old and new, some white-washed and others colourful.

Before a big house, with a little walled backyard, Paramjeet drew up. She matched the number-plate with the address she had got. Yes, that was where the controversial Professor of Palaeontology lived. Next to it was a smaller house with two young *jhau* (garden-pine) trees on either side of its gate.

They got down and pressed the bell. Out popped a bearded face, a shaggy head and a slightly bent framework.

"Have you got the 10 kilos of *palak saag*—- Oh, it's not the *sabziwallah*!"

The door was about to close on them when Madam Paramjeet boldly introduced herself and her students. She said she was guiding them in a school project on Palaeontology and so had to seek his guidance. "We are thrilled to have someone as famous as you living in Gurgaon. Please help us."

Professor Chakladar did not look too pleased.

"Can we come in, Sir, and waste a little of your precious time?" Deeksha spoke in a sweet tone. "That would be a great honour."

The professor opened the front door a little wider and they trooped in. It was a large sitting room but cluttered with tall shelves spilling over with books and a few potted plants. It was shaded with long green velvety curtains.

"It is a privilege to see you, Sir," said Anit.

"We have heard so much about you," chipped in Bimal.

"Hunh," snorted the professor. "Nasty things, I'm sure."

"Striking things, Sir," said Madam Paramjeet.

"Hunh," remarked the professor again. "Such as —?"

Before Paramjeet could say anything, Chandan blurted out, "Such as your claim that you could make dinosaurs come alive –"

"If only you could get hold of a dinosaur egg," put in Anit.

The professor looked at them coldly. "You have heard wrong," he said.

"Wrong, Sir?" faltered Madam Paramjeet.

"It is not that I *could* make a dinosaur come alive from an egg."

"No?"

"*I have already done so*," finished the professor.

For a moment, there was silence as the three of them, yes,

even Paramjeet, gaped. The professor suddenly burst into a cackle of laughter. "But how were you to know that! No one knows!" He lowered his voice to a whisper and added, "I haven't told a single soul."

"Can we – can we," Anit tried to get the words out.

"Yes, you can," said the professor. "Take a look, isn't that what you wanted to say?"

All of them nodded.

"Follow me," ordered the professor, "to the courtyard at the back." He got up with a bit of difficulty and led the way.

They followed him.

At the back of the house, there was a canopy of green netting. It was piled up with shrubs and creepers, ferns and fronds, and the hose-pipe had been left running to create humidity. At the far end, there was a huge water-tank.

"Take a look," the professor pointed to the water-tank.

Dinu

All of them looked into the water-tank and drew in their breath sharply. Half-submerged in the greenish waters was the most peculiar creature.

With leathery skin, ponderous body, long tail, and neck.

And a very mournful expression on its face.

"Dinu," Professor Chakladar called. "Dinu, the Dinosaur."

Anit saw the heap of grey leather stir, the droopy eyes open. The professor grinned. "See, it even responds to my call."

"But, but, why have you kept it hidden like this?" stuttered Madam Paramjeet. Anit too spoke out.

"Sir, you must tell the world! A real, live dinosaur! If, of course, —"

"Ah," said the professor. "There you are. If. If of course, it IS a dinosaur – Isn't that what you were about to say? —- Yes, that is all you can say!" he cried. "And that is all the world will say if I told it about Dinu. No, thank you. I have been through it before."

"But it is different this time. This time you have a real live creature to show it," persisted Paramjeet.

"Yes! Yes! We must tell everybody!" The ABCD spoke out together.

"One word more and I'll throw you all out," said the palaeontologist, looking quite livid.

Deeksha nudged Bimal and all of them shut up at once.

Madam Paramjeet changed the topic.

"But how did you get it. I mean this —-?"

"*Get* my Dinu? *Make* him, you mean," replied the professor.

"Make him?"

"Just that. I re-charged a dinosaur egg into life. Just as I had said I could. I am his creator."

"But where did you get the egg to start with?" Madam Paramjeet persisted.

"By the sheerest piece of luck," replied the professor. "I had decided to search and search and leave no stone unturned. But then, the stones turned themselves for me and I held the egg in my hand!"

Everyone was mystified.

"Sir, please will you clarify a little?" asked Paramjeet in a meek voice.

"That I will!" exclaimed the professor, expansively. "Come, let us go into the house and settle down in the drawing room. It is a long story."

They went in and settled down.

"Yet another yarn!"said Chandan under his breath.

"Shut up!" said Bimal, also under his breath.

In the Deccan

"You know, I am a native of Haryana but I have degrees even from abroad. I did have a prestigious faculty position and quite a bit of reputation, but that was before my unhappy experiences at the Palaeontology circuits of Delhi and Mumbai. Mad, that's what they had called me, all those highbrows of the world of science," began the professor.

"Yes, I've heard about that, Sir. A real shabby treatment you had got!" remarked Paramjeet.

"I had developed a formula for re-activating creatures with dinosaur genes and I needed to try it out. For that sort of experiment, you need a lot of funding. For laboratory, equipment and material on a large scale. Well, I could get no funds, only a lot of fun at my expense. I tried to work on my own. I travelled incognito in search of somewhere I could experiment upon some material, and I did come close to it. But then it turned out to be an unfortunate experience."

"It did not work, your formula?" asked Paramjeet.

"No, it did, or I think it did, but I could not be sure," the professor stopped abruptly, as if overcome by some horrible memory. "Why am I telling you all this!"

"Because we are with you, Sir," said Paramjeet. "We want to know and understand."

"Let me just tell you that after that disastrous experience I got totally frustrated. I threw away all my notes and formulae and even my scientific apparatus. I went on a different track. I gave up the pursuit of Western science and turned to Ayurveda. Was there anything in our ancient texts about the reversal of osmosis; some technique or chant to bring fossils back to life? You see, I have felt all along that Indians had in ancient times known how to bring back fossils to life. Rama, when he was reviving Ahalya was using – not any superpowers, but a technique the sages had taught him."

"But those are all stories," began Chandan.

"Not necessarily," said Paramjeet. "The *Ramayana* and the *Mahabharata* are also history. They are *Itihasa*, *Iti-ha-asa*, which means 'This is how it was."

"In *Vetala Panchavimshati* too there is a story of bones being brought to life," pointed out Bimal.

"Dadi once told me a Bengali folktale," said Anit, "where princes Arun and Barun were turned into stones and then revived by their sister, Princess Kiranmala."

"What about Satyajit Ray's story 'Professor Shonku and Bones'?" This was from Chandan.

"Right," said the professor. "You seem to have a lot more sense than those renowned scientists at the Congress. Well, in the course of my search – I don't see why I shouldn't call it research–I travelled up north. Gangotri in Uttarakhand is a celebrated pilgrim spot at the elevation of 3,100 metres. There I came across the great Ma Jeevanmoyee, the Mother who is Full of Life. I unburdened myself to her, I told her about my quest. In the beginning, she was reluctant to tell me anything. Then she told me that she had, in fact, come across such a *mantra* in an Ayurvedic text. She refused to tell me more. But when I pleaded and pleaded, she gave me a small pot of water over which she had chanted the *mantra*. But she still refused to tell me the lines. The ancient instructions bound her to secrecy. She could use her knowledge, but not impart it to anyone."

"But how did you know that it was THE thing you had been after?" asked Chandan. "Had you taken that Ma Jeevanmoyee entirely on trust?"

"Of course not, what do you take me for?" said the Professor

Chakladar indignantly.

"I had made Ma Jeevanmoyee demonstrate her powers to me. I had been carrying the small fossil of a leaf with me – just in case I struck upon something to my purpose. Now it came to use. Ma Jeevanmoyee sprinkled a drop of the liquid on it, and the plant sprung up green and fresh. Look there it is."

He pointed to a potted plant on one of his bookshelves. Everyone looked at it in awe. A potted plant more than 65 million years old!

"Sir, couldn't you have done a demonstration of it before people?" asked Chandan. His tone was polite but disbelieving.

"I did want to do it."

"Then?"

"They said that they did not want to host magic shows."

"Oh, that's not fair!" cried Anit, remembering Houdini and the simple magic he was teaching them. "Magic is not all hocus pocus. It is a skilful mix of art and science."

"I tried all I could to persuade the scientists I knew. Give me a chance, I said. But

"No," as one of them- named Professor Mohite–said. "'*Sci*' means 'to know'. If you cannot let us know your formula or method, we scientists have no place for you." That was when I started out on my own to hunt for dinosaur remains. Palaeontologist Jack Horner had in 1982 come upon a bed of ten thousand dinosaur fossils in Montana. Couldn't I do the same in the Deccan?"

"Why the Deccan?" asked Bimal.

."The Deccan plateau is ancient," the professor warmed up to his theme, "more ancient than the Himalayas. In his *Riddle of the Dinosaurs*, J.N Wilford has described how 65 million years ago, the very time the dinosaurs went extinct, there had been a massive upheaval in the Deccan making it a vast continental lava field. I thought perhaps there I could find there some material for my experiments – dinosaurs preserved in lava...

"I started following the course of the river Godavari from Nasik in Maharashtra. All I had with me was a big bag. It was gruelling, walking aimlessly like that. But I was much happier than I had been in the cities, in the exalted company of men who thought I was mad. The villagers were simpler and friendlier. The Deccan still had occasional earthquakes. But the villagers built back their homes every time. One evening–"

"Yes?" Everyone pressed forward.

"I was walking along a barren stretch when the ground right in front trembled and then yawned open."

"An earthquake!" exclaimed Paramjeet.

"Yes, a pretty strong one at that!" said Professor Chakladar. "And then?" gasped all three at once.

"When I recovered from shock, I saw that I had fallen into a much lower stratum of the earth. The soil was chalkish-grey. The sky far above was a tiny patch of indigo. The light was quickly fading and the high walls of stone and earth around me made it difficult to see anything around very clearly. I screamed for help, knowing full well that no one could come to my rescue there. And then –"

The listeners leaned forward.

"I looked more closely around. What were these objects, embedded in the walls around and the floor below? Huge bones? No, they couldn't be! But that one, it did look like a gigantic femur bone. And that, a collar bone, yes –."

Sitting in Bhondsi in Gurgaon, Anit felt as if he was down there in an ancient stratum of earth in the Deccan.

"I forgot that I was as good as dead. I only thought of the magnificent find I had made! And as I kept on looking around, the outlines of the fossils around me became clearer. I could see several dinosaur nests. I knew that dinosaurs were social creatures who built their nests in groups. Each nest was a hollow in the mud, about two meters across and one meter deep at the centre. In each nest, there was a clutch of eggs about twenty centimetres long, with the pointed ends buried in the hardened mud. Most of the eggs were smashed and broken. But one or two seemed to be intact. I touched one such egg and it seemed loose. Fossilized, but not stuck to the nest. Its surface was rough and ridged, but it seemed perfect and unbroken. I lifted up the egg and ecstatically pressed it to my chest."

"Huh!" said Chandan and turned it into "Han, Sir, go on, we're dying to hear the rest."

Professor Chakladar started again. "But how I would get out of the chasm with my treasure? I wondered but soon there was another tremor. This time, the earth below heaved up and thrust me back almost to the surface I had been walking along. It hurt but I clambered out while the chasm closed again. The dinosaur remains that had been exposed after 65 million years were buried once more. "

"And then?" asked Deeksha.

"With the dinosaur egg clutched to my chest I walked on till I found the nearest village. It had also felt some tremors last night and some of the huts and sheds had come down. But the damage was not severe, and the villagers could provide me shelter for a few days. Once rested, I wrapped my precious find in old rags from the village, and returned to Nasik, Mumbai, Delhi and eventually Bhondsi, my home."

"And then, didn't you tell everyone about your wonderful find?" asked Paramjeet.

The professor flew into a rage. "What, and be called a mad man again? What do you take me for? Really mad?"

Dinu's Diet

Suddenly, from the backyard came a strange sound. A sort of chirping, only hoarse.

"That's Dinu, calling out for food." They rushed to the backyard.

Sure enough, it was the creature in the tank. Raising his long neck, and squeaking hoarsely.

"Patience, patience," said the professor. He took up almost a kilogram of the palm fronds lying there in the backyard, and offered it to 'Dinu'.

He took it up in one gulp. Settling down into the tank, he began to chew. With a beatific expression on his face, he closed his eyes and drooled at the corners of his mouth.

"How sweet!" cried Deeksha.

"Is he plant-eating?" asked Anit.

"Yes, thank God, the egg I got happened to be of a species of herbivorous dinosaurs of the Brachiosaurus group. An Indian sauropod, known as Barapasauras Tagorei."

A-ha! They all recognised the name. Paramjeet thought of the femur bone in the glass case at the Museum of Natural History.

The Professor was going on. "Had I got the egg of a carnivorous dinosaur, I would have been in a fix. As it is, I am finding it difficult to provide Dinu all he needs."

"What *does* he need?" asked Anit.

"You see, he is a creature of swamps – the whole world was a swamp in his time and palm fronds and ferns were the only vegetation. So he wants a humid atmosphere and fronds and ferns to feed upon. That is not so easy to keep on supplying – especially as he wants more and more of it. I have asked all the vegetable vendors of the locality to bring loads of *palak* and other *saag*s to me. That's why when the bell rang I thought it was a *sabziwala*."

Dinu had finished his palm frond and was squeaking for more. Anit went forward and thrust some more into the tank. They were promptly snatched away. Then he felt a wet nose or muzzle pressing against him. Anit laughed. "Oh, Dinu's just like a puppy."

He had an idea. He would ask Padam to deliver an extra cart of greens here. Perhaps he could add Bhondsi to his circuit, or make some other arrangement? It would help Dinu get his feed.

"Sir, you haven't finished the whole story yet," said Chandan. "You got the egg, okay, but how did you get Dinu out of it?"

"Yes. Yes!" the rest of them clamoured.

"Another day," said their teacher. "Look, even though we live in Gurgaon, we live quite some distance away. I think we better make a move now."

"But we're dying to hear the end of the story," pleaded Anit.

"We'll come back as soon as we can," promised Paramjeet.

"Oh, alright," said the professor. "But, meanwhile, don't tell anyone about Dinu. Not a word."

The Day After

It was the toughest task for the ABCD not to tell anyone about what they had seen and heard at Bhondsi. But they did it and the day after, they turned up at the place again.

To their surprise, they found Dinu plodding about the drawing room. "He was getting a bit restless in the tank. So I let him out," said Professor Chakladar.

"He's quite hefty," observed Anit.

Dinu measured 4 feet across and his face, when he raised his neck, was about 5 feet from the floor. The tail itself was about 2 feet long. He raised it up as he caught sight of them, and brought it down on the floor with a heavy thud.

"He's happy to see us," said Bimal. "He's sort of wagging his tail," said Deeksha.

"We have got some ferns for him," said Paramjeet. She had spent quite a bit of her money on them. Ferns were plants that grew in profusion in prehistoric times and must be to Dinu's taste, she had thought.

Dinu seemed thrilled with them. He snatched them up from Paramjeet's hands, and settled down beside her.

"Now tell us, Sir," said Chandan. "What did you do after you got back here with the egg you had found in the Deccan?

"The first thing I did was close all the doors and windows of this room, take out the egg and unwrap it. Then I took out the pot of sanctified water Ma Jeevanmoyee had given me. I sprinkled a drop of the water on the egg."

"And?"

"And nothing happened. There was no reaction. I felt so let down. Had the liquid lost its potency? Had I been tricked? I turned the pot upside down and emptied it on the egg. I threw it away, turned off the light, and went away to my bedroom. After all, I was dead tired after all my travels."

"What a stench," cried Deeksha suddenly. It came from the spot where Dinu was quietly sitting beside Paramjeet and munching her ferns. The professor prodded him a little and he got up slowly. There was a huge brown mound below him. Dinosaur droppings!

"It is difficult to house-train a dinosaur," said the professor.

"It doesn't matter, Sir," laughed Deeksha and they all helped clear the mess away.

They noticed that Dinu was turning his long thick neck around and scratching his flanks.

"Are you itching, Dinu?" asked Bimal. "Feeling dry?"

Being winter it was cold but not perhaps humid enough for dinosaurs.

Dinu was taken to the hose-pipe. He closed his eyes in bliss as the water rained all over him. Then they trooped back to the drawing room. "Go on with your story, Sir," said Chandan. The professor frowned and he quickly said, "Your account."

"When I came into this room next morning, I saw the egg on the table where I had left it. Only it was no longer a fossil–a lifeless mass–an inanimate ellipsoid. It was –"

"An egg!" said everybody in unison.

"Yes, creamy in colour, with a rather thin shell. Even as I touched it, I could feel the life throbbing inside it. I checked it with an old stethoscope I happened to have. Sure enough, there was a heart beating inside."

Professor Chakladar had then put the egg in an improvised incubator–an earthen tub lined with clay and slush, like the nest it had been in. He had watched over it carefully. But nothing had happened for two whole months.

"Then suddenly one morning, I heard a loud pecking followed by a squeak. I rushed to the tub. Cracks had appeared on the surface of the egg and a head was peeping out. Then the quivering body came, with bits of shell clinging to it. The little thing looked like a lizard but it squeaked like a bird."

The professor had placed it in a huge carton lined with leaves shed with the approach of winter by the trees in his backyard. The baby had seemed quite comfortable there.

"I had realized that it belonged to a plant-eating species, I offered it some *palak saag*. But it was a toothless baby and couldn't chew it. I put it through the mixer, and that went down better."

Deeksha began to laugh.

"Fancy a mixer and a dinosaur going together! Why, they are ages apart!"

"But soon I didn't need the mixer anymore. In a fortnight, the baby grew little spoon-like teeth and learnt to chew. He could chew up bunches of *palak* in no time at all!"

"Could it walk properly?" asked Anit,

"At first, he sort of crawled. But after a week, he could balance itself on his four legs and toddle along. I kept a growth chart."

At that moment, there was a massive thumping of tail from Dinu who had been lumbering around the sitting- room. They turned towards him. Dinu gave an angry snort and grabbed hold of the green velvety curtains of the room.

"He's hungry and going after anything green!" exclaimed Anit.

"Not again!" said Professor Chakladar. "This is a big problem for me," he said to Paramjeet, shaking his head. "Dinu is a big eater."

He led Dinu to the larder next to his kitchen. This room had been entirely cleared of the rice, wheat, pulses and other provisions usually kept there. It was now stocked only with bundles of *saag*, cabbage, cauliflower, broccoli, ferns and palm fronds in their pots.

Dinu whinnied with delight at the sight.

"Have you informed Ma Jeevanmoyee about Dinu?" Paramjeet asked.

"I wrote to her as soon as Dinu was hatched. But I haven't heard from her in reply. I wonder if she is still in Gangotri or has moved to an even higher altitude."

"And have you done a lab analysis of any drops in the pot that could have been left?" Chandan queried. "How could I?" Professor Chakladar shouted. "Didn't I tell you that I had emptied out the pot on that egg? And then thrown it away?"

When they left for home, Dinu was still in the larder, feeding happily.

"Remember, not a word to anyone." The Professor repeated his warning.

Jaydeep Enters The Picture

By now the ABCD had got quite close to their class-teacher and on getting back to their own sector in Gurgaon, went in there for some evening snacks with her. She lived by herself in a studio apartment not too far from the school. They told her about Houdini, and Anit shared an idea that had occurred to him.

"I have heard that all dinosaurs are not extinct. Some of them had adjusted with the changing climate and changed themselves. Some evolved into birds and some into reptiles, both egg-laying creatures like the dinosaurs. Did the ancient sages know this? Was the Kadru-Vinata story a symbolic way of their saying so?"

"Could be." said Paramjeet. "There is so much in Indian mythology that is logical and scientific."

But before any discussion could proceed, Jaydeep drew up on his motorcycle. "Paramjeet, I've brought you some roses," he said. Anit saw that he had got rid of his pony-tail and his rough manners. He greeted Anit with a friendly salute and was duly introduced to the others.

"Aren't you going to thank me for bringing you roses?" he said lightly to Paramjeet.

."They are lovely. But I wish you had bought some spinach instead."

"Why on earth?" Jaydeep was taken aback.

"Then I could have taken it to Dinu tomorrow," said Paramjeet, foolishly, as Anit thought. Why, he had kept the matter a secret from his parents although he had been tempted to consult them. From Houdini too, who was now part of the family.

But the fat was in the fire. "Who's Dinu?"

Jaydeep swooped down and got everything out of them. Well, he did have a claim to the information. After all, it was he who had got them the professor's address.

It was difficult to make Jaydeep believe in Dinu.

First, he laughed. Then he sniggered, and finally he said, "Well, 'seeing is believing' and I will not believe until I see."

"But we saw Dinu with our own eyes, Jaydeep," said Paramjeet.

"That's what you say," taunted Jaydeep.

"Okay, next time we go there, you come along with us," said Anit. "But mind you, this is not for the press."

"Of course! I will sup-press it completely," Jaydeep attempted a pun. "By the way, how is that pup I almost ran over?"

Perhaps Jaydeep was a changed man ....thought Anit.

Jaydeep Meets Dinu

The next weekend, they went to Bhondsi by taxi and that too, with Jaydeep instead of Paramjeet. Her car was in a garage being serviced, and there was some other work that she could not get out of. But Jaydeep was so keen on going that Paramjeet suggested that her students go by themselves and take Jaydeep along. They knew the way and she would explain it to their parents who were under the impression that their children were going with their teacher on a school project.

"But the professor will be disgusted with us when we tell him that we have brought a newspaper reporter with us," Anit pointed out.

"Well, don't tell him then," said Jaydeep. "I am not carrying my video camera or anything, am I, to give the show away?"

The reached Bhondsi and the professor's house. The taxi, taken on an hourly basis from the local taxi-stand, would wait.

The professor had frowned when he had seen Anit and others, that too, without Madam Paramjeet. His frown had deepened when he had seen Jaydeep also stepping in. Anit began on an introduction but Jaydeep cut in, "I am Dr. Jaydeep Pradhan."

The professor's frown cleared.

"That's a godsend," he exclaimed. "I am glad you have brought him along. You see, Dinu's got hurt. I need a vet for him but how can I call in anyone without letting him on to the secret. I am glad you have, well, done what you shouldn't have. Come, this way..."

"I am not a vet, Sir," said Jaydeep, attempting a false dignity to get out of being exposed.

"But you are a doctor, aren't you? You *will* be able to do something. Come, let me take you straight to the bathroom."

"The bathroom, Sir?"

"Yes, that's where I have kept Dinu now."

In the spacious green-tiled bathroom, in a huge bath-tub now lined with clay and filled with water, reposed Dinu.

Jaydeep looked at him, and then slowly sank down on his knees, right on the floor.

Dinu shuffled a little and that splattered water all over Jaydeep but he didn't even notice.

He just stared at Dinu. Reverently.

"The scoop of the year!" He said softly.

"I beg your pardon?" said the professor from the back. Jaydeep pretended not to hear. He went on to a thorough examination of Dinu's physique. He touched him and felt him and pressed him and even pinched him. Then he let out a whistle under his breath. "He's real!" The others grinned at one other. So Jaydeep was impressed!

The professor began to tell them how Dinu had injured himself.

"Yesterday Dinu was walking about the room when he bumped against the shelf, and the whole thing came crashing down on him. He couldn't stand up by himself at first, and even now he keeps on lying down."

Indeed, they all saw that Dinu was lying in a heap today, with his back sometimes arching as if in pain.

"Poor Dinu," said Deeksha and stroked his soft leathery forehead.

Dinu opened his eyes and nuzzled against Deeksha's hands.

Jaydeep made a further pretence of examining him.

"Do something for him fast," said the professor impatiently. "He's in great pain."

"Yes, Sir, let's get him some benzodiazepines or paracetamols! Quick!"

The professor nodded eagerly.

"About twenty will do for the first dose. The number must be in proportion to the body-weight. Oh no!" Jaydeep broke off mid-way. "I am not carrying my writng pad with the letter-heads – I left it at home."

"Oh, I don't think your letter-head is necessary for two sheaves of pain-killers." The professor said at once. "I am quite well-known at the local chemist's shop, for buying pain-killers for an old injury of mine." He rushed out to get the brand of pain-killer Jaydeep had suggested. Immediately Jaydeep got his Smartphone out of his pocket and took a few shots of Dinu.

''You can't do that," said Anit.

"Well, I already have," said Jaydeep. "That's mean, real mean," said Deeksha.

"You don't mean it, do you?"said Jaydeep. "Sorry for the pun but watch your words with me. Shall I tell your parents what you are doing without their permission? Behind their back?"

"But you *had* promised us that this would not go to the press," Anit, Bimal and Chandan spoke out. "Oh, don't worry about that," Jaydeep said. "This is only for myself."

The professor was back with the pills.

Dinu looked puzzled as he held out the twenty shining pills in his hand, gave a massive snort, and turned his head away.

"Put them in a bunch of *palak*," suggested Deeksha.

That proved successful. Once stuffed within a bunch of spinach, the pills went easily into Dinu. In a few minutes, he opened his mouth and let out a half-groan half-yawn. Then his eyes closed and he fell into a slumber.

Jaydeep observed with a very serious face, "Well, that was only to kill the pain. For actual treatment, I must have a proper investigation done. Especially as this is a species unknown. "

He paused and said dramatically, "I am afraid he has got a fractured spine."

"Poor thing!" exclaimed Deeksha, quite forgetting Jaydeep's credentials or, rather, the lack of them for making any such pronouncement.

"But I cannot be sure," went on Jaydeep, "without an X-Ray being done."

"An X-Ray! But then he'll have to be taken to a Radiologist!" said Professor Chakladar.

"Well, only for his own good," said Jaydeep.

Anit muttered to Bimal, "I don't like this at all. That Jaydeep must have something up his sleeve!"

"Yes, I'm sure he means mischief," agreed Bimal.

"But after all, Dinu *is* hurt and he's got to have proper treatment," said Deeksha.

"Sharma Uncle is there ..." began Chandan.

"But he is too far away," said Anit.

They swathed Dinu in a Kashmiri shawl of the professor's, and somehow carried him out to the taxi on wait. The driver offered his help but they refused it. "Just hurry," ordered Jaydeep. "Can't you see we have got a patient with us?"added the professor. Dinu settled his huge body into their laps. He was too sleepy to protest.

Dinu Under The X-Ray

Bhondsi did have a Primary Health Centre but Jaydeep would settle only for a diagnostic centre. So they went back more than half the way to a small diagnostic centre in Badshapur itself. Paramjeet, Bimal, Chandan and Deeksha, along with the professor, waited in the taxi with Dinu, still covered in the shawl, while Anit and Jaydeep went in.

Jaydeep called the radiologist aside and whispered something to him. Anit saw him pass the man a wad of notes. The man looked astonished but nodded. Jaydeep went out at once and called the others in. Anit saw them bring Dinu in, still draped in the shawl. As Dinu was brought out of the depths of the shawl, the man's mouth opened in a round 'O'.

"What animal is this?" he asked shakily. "Didn't you get more than the standard dues? Just do your job," responded Jaydeep in a voice of authority. The man quickly fell to work. Dinu was carried to the room where the X-Ray machines were, and the radiologist locked the door from inside. Once the door opened, Dinu was brought out in his draping and loaded on to the taxi. Everybody piled in, everybody other than Jaydeep. He was talking to the radiologist.

"The X-Ray report will take a little while," the radiologist was saying. "That's all right," Jaydeep told him.

"Just hand me the X-Ray plate; I'll rush with it to a doctor I know. "

He turned to the taxi-driver and asked him to first go back to the house they had just visited and then take Anit and the others back. Being from the local taxi-stand, the man readily agreed, especially as Jaydeep gave him his payment then and there, and an extra wad – with a pat on his back.

Then he hailed a passing auto-rickshaw and was gone!

"B-but...," Deeksha began to protest, "he can't leave us like this!"

"He has!" said Chandan.

"Let him!" said Bimal."We'll manage without him."

"Of course," said Anit, not to be out-done.

The taxi started off.

On the return journey, Dinu began to stir. It became a tough job to keep him under the shawl. Once back, he was relieved of the shawl and taken to the bathroom.

The professor put him back into the tub, turned the shower softly on, and thrust some greens before him.

Then the taxi went back, dropping everyone at their respective homes.

Dino Out Of the Bag

Next morning the dinosaur was out of the bag. The Barapasaurus was all over the newspapers, local as well as a few national ones.

"A Dinosaur in Bhondsi," "Extinct Creature Brought to Life," "Palaeontologist's Claim," "Jurassic Hoax" ... the headlines screamed. Under the headlines there were photographs of a curious creature with an X-Ray of its bone structure. The print was, in general, bad and the pictures blurred. But there was no mistaking it. It was Dinu in flesh and blood as well as in complete skeletal form.

Baba saw it first as he picked up the morning paper from the doorstep. "Must be a hoax ...an instance of trick photography," he said as he passed it on to Ma.

Anit too saw the news and screamed out:

"So that's what Jaydeep had rushed off to do, as soon as he had got the X-Ray done. Gone to the Press!"

"What ARE you talking of, Anit?" said Baba and Ma and soon got the whole story out of him.

"I am sure the media is there now, hounding the creature out," said Baba.

There were knocks at the door. Mr. Nath had come over with his paper to be read out before Anit went off to school. "It seems there is some incredible news today – right from Gurgaon!"

As Anit read it out to him in trembling tones, there were door-bells. Why, it was Madam Paramjeet. Obviously hurriedly dressed, she had come over to pick Anit up. "Let him skip school today," she pleaded with Baba and Ma. "I'll explain later but now I need him to come with me."

Paramjeet's car had come back from the garage last evening, and she had already picked Bimal, Chandan and Deeksha up from their houses which she knew as she had dropped them at their places earlier.

Baba and Ma nodded though they looked quite bewildered. Anit rushed out and got into the car.

"That Ponytail!" he found Chandan saying, "He betrayed us."

"Ponytail? Oh, you mean Jaydeep? Yes, has betrayed us all," said Paramjeet.

"He had promised us not to leak the news and he did," Anit felt close to tears.

"Oh, why did we ever tell him anything?" Bimal cried.

"Any way," Deeksha said soothingly, "let's go and see what's happening with Dinu."

Dinu Under The Public Eye

Paramjeet drove as fast as she could. As they sped past Badshapur and reached Bhondsi, they saw that a small crowd had gathered outside Professor Chakladar's house. Inquisitive neighbours had gathered there, as well as reporters and photographers. There were cars with PRESS marked on them and a van with a television unit.

The professor was refusing to let anyone in. Everyone was refusing to go away.

"You have to let us in!" shouted a man with a camera.

"Allow us a glimpse," the television crew was pleading.

"Certainly not," shouted Professor Chakladar, holding the gate fast.

When he saw Anit and the others with Paramjeet, he turned purple in the face. "You traitors and betrayers! How dare you show your faces here!"

"Sir, it wasn't us who went to the Press," they defended themselves.

"That was Jaydeep," said Paramjeet.

"But you were the ones who had brought Jaydeep over here," shouted the professor. "So it is all your fault. You idiots! You don't know what you have done." But he did open the gate and let them in. Along with the crowd.

Bombarding them with questions, the crowd followed them to the bathroom. As they saw Dinu in his tub, there were exclamations and questions again. Some of them had Smart phones and started taking photographs and making recordings.

"Do you notice something?" said Anit. "Dinu seems to have grown bigger!"

"And he's come out in rashes," observed Bimal. True enough, Dinu's body, a grey expanse, was seething with pink and white boils. "Has he had reactions to the pills, do you think?" Chandan asked.

Meanwhile, the professor was still trying to keep the crowd at bay.

"Clear out! I won't answer a single question more!"He looked so fierce that the crowd dispersed. Anyway, they had got their looks at Dinu and their photographs and video-recordings.

Only one man still hung around. A very prosperous-looking man with an even more prosperous-looking tummy.

"I am Rangalal, businessman and builder. The builder of all the houses and apartments in Bhondsi-Badshapur. Even this one. I have a business proposition for you. I want to buy up your animal," he said to Professor Chakladar.

The professor clenched his fists as if to hit Rangalal. But at that very moment, there was a crash from inside and the door to the sitting-room fell apart as Dinu charged into it.

Only yesterday, he had been just as tall as the low centre-table. Anit saw that he was now as tall as the door! Wasn't the growth rate abnormal, even for a dinosaur?

He pushed at the professor with his muzzle.

"He's hungry," said Anit. "But haven't you already had your breakfast, Dinu!" By now the ABCD knew their way about the house, and led Dinu to the larder. But where was its stock of dinosaur delicacies such as cabbages, cauliflowers, broccoli, lettuce, pine needles, and ferns? Today it was almost empty except for a few pale cabbages.

"Finish the leftovers, Dinu," said Chandan, patting his back.

Once back in the sitting-room, they found a hot fight going on. "Get out at once!" The professor was shouting at Rangalal. "I won't sell Dinu to you even if you pay me 10 lakhs!"

"Dinu is not for sale," Paramjeet shouted indignantly. "How dare you even suggest such a thing!"

"What about 12 lakhs then," Rangalal belched out, passing a hand across his tummy.

"But why? Why do you want to buy Dinu up?" asked Paramjeet. "What do you intend to do with him?"

"Business. I want to sell him to a business contact of mine. He has a travelling circus of odd creatures and deformed animals. A five-legged calf, a two-headed deer, Siamese twins, — you know. Dinu will be a crowd-puller."

The professor lunged at him. Anit held him back. Wordlessly Paramjeet held the door open for him. Rangalal left. But at the gate, he turned and smiled, "Think it over. 15 lakhs."

The ABCD knew that it was cruelty to display defective or abnormal specimens - human or animal - to the public and get money for such shows. But it goes on in India. Rangalal would be able to make a fortune out of Dinu. It was essential to protect Dinu from that sort of exploitation.

But there was another more immediate issue! "Sir, sir, Dinu has finished all the stuff in the larder and is asking for more!"

The professor clutched his head in despair.

There was a fresh spate of insistent knocks on the door. "That Rangalal again! Just don't open the door," said the professor.

But Paramjeet peeped out and said: "No, Sir. It's not that fellow. I recognise some old professors of mine. Why, the entire intellectual world has got to know of your discovery and come to pay tributes."

"No!" cried the professor in dismay.

It may not have been the entire intellectual world, but at least some venerable heads that Paramjeet knew from her university days. "That's Dr. Mohite of the Archaeological Survey, and that's

Dr. Seshanathan of the Department of Ancient Indian History and Culture. And that lady is Dr. Mundle, Professor Emeritus, the Department of Geology."

Anit saw several serious-looking elderly men and a thin, elderly lady.

There were others as well. Professor Keshavan of Botany and Professor Roy of Biology. "We can't send them back from the door, Sir," said Paramjeet.

Professor Chakladar opened the front door with a very bad grace.

"What have you great people come here for?" he asked. "To call me names again?" But at the sight of Dinu, 'the great people' were too taken up with him to retort. As they drew closer to Dinu, the professor shouted "Stay off!" but they ignored him and kept on advancing.

Deeksha could not check herself when they actually began to touch Dinu. "Hands off!" she cried. But Anit saw that the professors did not seem to hear.

After a couple of pokes and prods from them, Dinu gave a swipe of his tail that made them reel back.

Now they turned upon the professor.

"We congratulate you on your find," began Professor Mohite.

"More than a find," said the professor. "A creation." He came out with his account of how he found a fossilized dinosaur egg in the Deccan and brought it to life through the aid of Ayurveda.

Anit and others saw the guests trying not to smile. No, they did not laugh away the matter of Dinu's creation, but they put the matter in an altogether different light.

"Now that you have made this fantastic find, Professor, do you understand that you cannot keep him with you like this?"said Dr. Mohite.

"You will have to make alternative arrangements for him," said Dr. Roy.

"Hand over the charge to some institution like The

Archaeological Survey or The Geological Survey?" said Dr. Mundle. "But Dinu isn't merely an archaeological find from under the earth. He's a living and breathing creature in our midst," replied the professor.

"But then, what about the Zoological Park?" It was Professor Mohite again.

"The Zoo!" shouted the professor. "For children to come and peer in through the bars!"

"You will have to do some such thing, you know. Make other arrangements. You can't possibly cope by yourself."

"I can, thank you."

"What is the creature's height?"

"He is a six-footer."

"Already! And how much does he weigh?"

"About 90 kg."

"And how old is he exactly?"

"Three months, one week."

"Do you realize, my dear professor, that by the time he is full-grown he will be about 60 feet tall and weigh 20 tons?"

Anit drew in his breath sharply.

The professor paused for a moment and then said defiantly: "So what? That is the normal measure of a Brachiosaurus or Barapasaurus."

"My dear professor, how will you take care of him then? Where will you keep him? How will you feed him?"

"I'll manage somehow."

"It will be quite beyond you," said Dr. Mohite. "Why don't you admit it?" piped in Dr. Seshanathan. "I'll think about it when the time comes. At present I am perfectly able to cope," said the professor.

But Dinu did seem to be getting out of hand!

His head reached beyond the tallest of the bookshelves. His tail swept the far end of the room. His massive abdomen and neck loomed above their heads.

"No, professor, that will not do." The visitors got up to go.

"We will not let the matter rest here. We are going to call an Executive Committee meeting of the Science Society and take it up there."

"I don't see how you can. This is my personal matter and you have thrown me out of the Society years back."

"That is where you are making the mistake, professor. Whether or not you are a member of the intellectual community, your discovery is a matter of interest to it," said Professor Mohite.

Suddenly Dinu swung his neck towards him. He drooled green masticated stuff all over his white hair and clean shirt. Professor Mohite shot out of the house. The others hastily followed.

Once outside, they shouted, "You'll hear from us again," "We'll call an emergency meeting of the Congress," and so on.

But there was no time to pay attention to them.

Inside, Dinu had gone on a rampage. He was stamping upon the furniture, swiping at the books on the shelves, and whinnying again and again.

"What's the matter, Dinu?" Paramjeet stroked his flanks, all she could reach now.

There was a hollow rumble from Dinu's stomach.

"He's hungry," said she.

"But that's absurd! That's impossible!" said Professor Chakladar. "He's just had five tons of *sabzi*."

"Sir, don't you find something odd in the way he is growing?" asked Paramjeet. "Isn't it too fast?"

The professor mopped his forehead. "Just what I have been thinking, but was afraid to admit."

"Maybe dinosaurs grow fast?" suggested Anit.

"Yes. After all, we do not know much about them," said Bimal.

"No, kids," said the professor sadly. "If anything, their growth

metabolism was very slow. They grew slower though they grew bigger and lived far longer."

Paramjeet had a green *shawl* on. Dinu pulled at it began to chew on it. "Oh-oh-oh Dinu, that's not your food, even though it's green," laughed Paramjeet. Dinu himself had discovered the bitter truth. For, he spat the fabric out and squeezed himself out through the front door. He lumbered out into the pocket-sized lawn in the front. His huge elephant-like legs made deep dents on the grass. His tall neck swayed on either side.

He sniffed at the bricks of the wall, and then at the twin garden pine trees on the other side. Easily he reached one of them, squealed with delight and began to chew on it.

"Dinu, stop, it's the neighbour's," Paramjeet thumped Dinu's flanks. Dinu did not seem to even feel it.

The professor watched Dinu with an affectionate expression. "See, how he is relishing it. You see, in their times, the coniferous trees were, more or less, the only sort on earth. Trees like mango and jamun had not appeared. Or, for that matter, flowers and even grass –"

But the professor could not finish. There was an yell from inside the next house. The lady next door had caught sight of Dinu starting on her second garden pine. She ran out. She must have been cooking. For, she had a wooden spatula in her hand. "You monster, you devil!"

"Madam, I can explain," the professor tried to say weakly. But Dinu chewed up the second tree as well, and took a swipe at the spatula in the lady's hand. The next moment, he was chewing it up and the lady was running away.

A voice rung out from across the road. "20 lakhs!" Rangalal had not given up. He had been hanging around.

The professor lost his cool. He flung open his gates and tried to go out after Rangalal. But his bent spine prevented him from going fast.

The gate was made of wood. Dinu chewed up the whole thing and then rushed on to the open road.

Dinu Hits The Road

"Stop, Dinu," cried Anit and ran after him. So did Bimal, Chandan and Deeksha. The professor gave up chasing Rangalal and came rushing back to chase Dinu. So did Rangalal.

Paramjeet ran to her car and took the professor up in it. Ahead of them lumbered Dinu. Along the Main Sohna Road and towards Gurgaon. Leaving the Aravali range behind and moving through households and shops, walls and vehicles. Once he crashed against an old brick wall and brought it down. Another time he stooped to drink water that had collected in the cement rings kept on the ground for being joined to make underground pipes. From either side, people came to join the chase.

Paramjeet could not pick up speed. "Quick! Someone, call the Bhondsi Police Station!" she cried. "I can't for I am at the wheel." Anit and the others had no cell phones but as they ran after Dinu, they shouted out to the people around. "The police! Someone call the police!" "No," the professor shouted at the same time: "No, no!"

But a few had already called the Gurgaon police and soon the shrill notes of the police siren were heard.

Immediately Dinu broke into a run. The locals were busy at their respective jobs, or simply enjoying their leisure. An old man was lying on a charpoy puffing at his hookah. At Dinu's sudden emergence, they were thrown into a flurry. The old man even fell off his charpoy. A few men began to pick up broken bricks and shards lying around, and pelt Dinu with them. By now Dinu had rashes all over. The pelting made him shriek in agony.

Padam was seen in the distance, coming from Gurgaon with a cartload of greens. Pappu was also there, in Chhaya's coat. Dinu sniffed at the air and turned towards him. But before he could reach the greens, Pappu broke out from Padam and charged at him. Full as he was of sores and cuts, Dinu faced Pappu squarely.

But the police van arrived just then. People scattered away, not to speak of Pappu with Padam after him. Scooters and cycles, autos and cars ... all cleared away. But Dinu stood there, unmoving. Was he scared? Or just confused? The van moved towards him and he lashed his tail upon it. Part of the bonnet crumpled up like a paper carton.

There was the roar of a motor-cycle from the direction of Gurgaon. It came right up to the middle of the road as if to block Dinu's way. Jaydeep jumped down, unstrapped his video-camera and targeted Dinu.

"Move away, you idiot!"cried Paramjeet from her car. "Don't you have any sense?"

Chandan ran up to Jaydeep and tried to pull him back. But even before he could, Dinu had dipped his neck and snatched up – no, not Jaydeep himself – but his video-camera. "Give it back! Hey, give it back!" shouted Jaydeep. But Dinu was in no mood to do so. Shaking his head and arching his neck, he dangled it tantalisingly before Jaydeep. Then he flung it far away on one side. "It's fallen into that old *baoli*," called out a local fellow, and Jaydeep rushed away to get it back from an old step-well, fallen into disuse and choked up with weeds. "He is never going to get his video-camera back," tittered another bystander. "I am glad," thought Anit. "It is he who brought all this upon us."

Meanwhile, the policemen had got down from the van and were trying to calm the local people down. "*Shant rahiye,*" they were announcing on their loudspeaker. The ABCD joined them, saying:

"Look, don't hit him. He's not going to eat you up."

"He is herbivorous. That is, *shakahari*. Not interested in non-veg!"

"But what animal *is* this?" Everyone kept on saying. "Never seen such a creature!"

The terms 'Brachiosaurus', 'Barapasaurus' or even 'Dinosaur' made no sense to them. Professor Chakladar was also shouting to the people from Paramjeet's car while Paramjeet herself focussed on inching ahead. "Don't harm him. He is a creation of mine. I gave him his life. From an egg that was 65million years old. He is a priceless asset to science."

"*Pagal hai kya* (Mad, is he)?" the locals were saying to one another even as they gaped at the strange creature before them or threw splinters and shards at it.

Anit saw one of the policemen – must be an officer–take out a Pistol Auto and aim it at Dinu.

"Don't, Sir," he screamed. "The professor is right. Dinu is a marvel. He is a dinosaur come to life. An extinct species re-born."

"He is a public nuisance, whatever he is," barked out the police officer.

"That's because he is hungry and sick and scared himself," said Chandan. "Otherwise he is a quiet little – well, not quite little – creature."

"If you shoot him, it will be an irreparable loss to the world," said Bimal.

"You will not forgive yourself and nor will the world," added Anit.

"Well, then let's wait for the Zoo officers to come with their tranquilizers," said he. "The Delhi Zoo being a long way off, they will take some time in coming. But I will inform the authorities." He put his pistol away, and spoke into his walkie-talkie. Then he again had it announced on the loudspeaker that there was no need to panic. "The Zoo authorities have been informed and officials are coming with their tranquilizers. One shot and this creature will be quiet."

The professor got down from Paramjeet's car and lumbered

up to the police van. He grabbed the loudspeaker and spoke into it: “He will be quiet even now without any shots. Just don’t provoke him, that is all. He is docile, I tell you. Like a cow or a buffalo. I appeal to you. Don’t get him worked up. Let him relax.”

The ABCD too shouted, “Just let him be.”

Others Come Along

But before this announcement could have a chance of working, there came a car from the direction of Gurgaon. A most familiar car. It moved slowly and carefully through the crowd and then drew up to one side. Three people got out. Anit saw it was Baba and Ma, and Houdini. How did they get to know what was happening here?

At the sight of Dinu, they stood stock-still and staring. But Anit called out to them and went up to them as fast as he could.

"That's Dinu. He is only three months old but actually, he is 65 million years old."

"Yes, yes, we saw the papers...Only we never knew you had any link with this," said Ma. "But the way your teacher had picked you up this morning, I put two and two together and called your father at his office."

"I had happened to come to your place today soon after you left," said Houdini. "I took the chance to come along. *He He He He*! This is better than any road show I could ever put up. Better than any magic I could have worked."

"It's not a show, Houdini, it is real," said Anit.

"I have no words for it. Well, we have taken a look at Dinu. Now take us to the Dinu's maker." Anit began to steer the three of them towards the professor. But as Houdini caught a glimpse of the professor's face, he gave a massive start. "That's... that's ...!" He could hardly get the words out. The professor too had happened to see Houdini that instant.

"You here!" spluttered the professor.

"You here!" roared Houdini. They walked towards each other – both slowly – and gripped each other. Neither wanted to let the other go.

"Houdini," Anit asked. "Do you know Professor Chakladar—?"

"Chakladar, my foot! He is Bhide – the Dr.Bhide I met in Goa."

Baba and Ma looked bewildered while the ABCD gasped. The professor was squirming in Houdini's grasp. "Don't let him go," cried Houdini. "You ran away at Goa. This time, you shall not escape!"

A part of the crowd had by now gathered around them. A policeman came up and asked:

"What's all this? Someone picking someone's pocket – but which one and whose pocket?"

At that Houdini left the professor and turned to the policeman, "Do I look like a pick-pocket?"

The policeman laughed and looked him up and down. Indeed, Houdini looked an odd figure, even without his blue spangled robe. Scraggy and shabby.

But so did the professor, red-eyes and trembling.

Anit looked at them face to face. Was the professor an evil man then, a pretender, a confidence-trickster? But then wasn't the magician a trickster as well, creating delusion in people's minds?

But what was Dinu then? A trick or fact? Illusion or reality? Standing there – right there- in a world that had ceased to be his, since 65 million years? Under a sun that was never meant to shine upon him?

Someone Else

Before Anit could resolve his conflict, there was a new commotion.

Yet someone else was coming.

Neither rushing nor pushing. The crowd was moving away on either side to let her pass.

An elderly lady with snow-white hair, but so different from Dr. Mundle, the scientist who had visited Professor Chakladar and who could have been of similar age.

She was barefoot and in a red-bordered sari. Her forehead was anointed in sandalwood and vermillion. She wore a rosary of *rudraksha* berries and carried a *lota* or *kamamdalu* (metal pitcher with a long curved spout and a handle on top).A *jhola* made of cloth hung from one shoulder.

As the professor caught sight of him, he somehow broke away from Houdini and reached up to her.

With folded palms, he cried: "So you got my letter."

"I did," smiled the lady, "in spite of your just addressing it to Ma Jeevanmoyee, Gangotri, without any other particulars. It went to a couple of other temples and monasteries before it got passed on to me. I decided to descend at once, and come to your place – to the address you had put in the letter."

"I had written to you as soon as Dinu had been born. Look at him now. There he stands and only by your blessings."

Jeevanmoyee Ma turned her eyes to the spot where Dinu stood with the rest of the crowd. He was trying to scratch himself with his forelegs but not with success as being herbivorous he had no hooked nails. He was also trying to rub his sores – boils that had burst, and wounds that stones and bricks had inflicted. From time to time, he stretched his neck and whinnied, an inarticulate cry for aid. From time to time, he shuffled and the crowd round him fell back with mock cries of fear. Someone from a safe distance tempted him with a long leafy branch but snatched it away as soon as Dinu dipped to get at it. The crowd sniggered. Dinu dipped lower and grabbed the branch. He raised his neck and began to chew its leaves. The crowd clapped.

Jeevanmoyee Ma looked at him for a while before speaking: "I knew I needed to come down, and as soon as reached Delhi, I saw today's newspapers .I knew then that I was just in time."

"Help Dinu, Ma," the professor burst out. "Save Dinu from being mobbed by the ignorant public, from being displayed by greedy businessmen, and being dissected by unfeeling scientists."

The ABCD folded their palms and echoed, "Save Dinu from all this."

Dinu Back To Form!

Jeevanmoyee Ma took some water from her *lota* in her hands, and began to chant:

"*Aum Shileebhuto Punarbhava*

Aum Purvarupa Punarbhava"

"No!" cried Anit and the others. They could make out the meaning. They had started on Sanskrit at school.

But Jeevanmoyee Ma went on chanting and sprinkling the water high so that it could fall on Dinu, but not any others. The droplets cut shining curves in the air as they caught the sunlight. They touched Dinu. He gave a moan and stopped munching. The branch that he had been munching fell from his mouth. But he did not try to bend and pick it up.

Jeevanmoyee Ma went on chanting and sprinkling.

"Go back to stone again,

Back to your own form again."

Dinu stood still. A faint whinny started out from his throat and died before it reached the now stiff but gaping mouth.

The chanting and sprinkling went on, and Dinu's complexion began to change to ashen-grey. The blood and pus trickling out of his sores stopped in their courses. The throbbing of the underbelly began to slow down. The tail lashed down once more and then fell limp. The body began to shrink and shorten.

“What are you doing to my Dinu!” The professor fell at Jeevanmoyee’s feet. People surged around Dinu, jostling one another.

Dinu’s forelegs stiffened and his hind legs huddled together.

The professor left Jeevanmoyee’s feet and hurled himself upon Dinu. He put his arms round him. He beat his head upon the changing mass that Dinu had become. “Dinu, *beta*, come on, move your legs, thrash your tail. Don’t give up like this.”

But the chanting went on and right before everyone’s eyes Dinu’s body shrunk and changed shape. The head, neck, forelegs, hind legs and tail–all seemed to fold up under the abdomen. Individual parts seemed to melt and mix into one shape –

Anit could see the shape emerging even before it had actually formed.

Yes, it was an ellipsoid. More simply, an egg.

He went up and touched it tenderly. But even under his touch, the leathery surface with its contents thickened, hardened and solidified.

Dinu had been literally turned to stone, that is, petrified. He was again in the form in which he had been discovered in the Deccan. A fossil.

“Dinu, my poor Dinu,” wailed the professor.

“Ashes to ashes, dust to dust. And now it is stone to stone,” Houdini put his arms round him. He still held him close but now he was trying to comfort him.

Deeksha was openly crying and Anit himself felt like crying.

By then a van had driven in with a team of vets and Zoo attendants. One of them had a gun to anesthetize the strange creature they had been called in for. Another had an injection syringe. The team was sent back but then there arrived a team of reporters and officials. The scientists too were back. They wanted to see if a DNA test could still be done. There were heated discussions as to where the egg would be taken. The National Museum? The Archaeology Department? The Zoology Department? The Geology Department? Delhi? Bombay?

Kolkata? Taken as what? What would it be the name of the 'entry' wherever it went?

The National Museum was the immediate choice. Thereafter, the governments would sit and deliberate upon the matter.

When the professor was asked as a matter of courtesy, he bawled: "Take it away. Give it to the government. I found it underground and by law, it belongs to the government. If the government hands it over to scientists, let them decide. My Dinu is gone. That ellipsoid object is not Dinu."

Government officials arrived in their car and took possession of the ellipsoid. As they drove off with Dinu-turned-into-an-egg, the professor covered his eyes up. Anit too found the sight unbearable.

The Order Of Things

Broken as he was, the professor pleaded with Ma Jeevanmoyee to accompany him into his house. "It was on my invitation that you came," he said. "Whatever you have done for my sake – however it hurts – you have to be my guest."

But Ma Jeevanmoyee refused smilingly. "I have another promise to keep. I have to see an old friend of mine. She has been ailing for a long time and asking me to pay her a visit. She stays in Gurgaon. So I can combine that visit with this – now that there is nothing here for me to do. Do any of you know where this would be?" She took out a letter from her *jhola* and read out an address.

"Why, it is very close to us!" said Ma.

"I'll take you there," said Baba. "I'll be honoured."

Anit too marvelled at the coincidence. So Mrs. Nath was Jeevanmoyee Ma's friend from college days just as she had been Dadi's childhood friend! The crowd was now fast dispersing. "*Kya tamasha hua*!" They were saying to one another. Indeed it had been quite a spectacle for quiet Badshapur.

Paramjeet did not let the professor go back alone to his place. "I'll tidy up the place for you, Sir, and see that there is some dinner for you. Bimal and Deeksha, you stay back with me and help clear the mess. I will drop you home later when I leave."

Anit and Chandan piled in with Baba, Ma, Houdini and Jeevanmoyee Ma.

As Baba had rung up the Naths in between, they were fully prepared for their visit. Mrs. Nath had left her bed and she was waiting at the door, holding on to son Vinod. She made a move as if to hug Jeevanmoyee Ma, but she had to be content with a sprinkling from the *lota*, and a muttering of some *mantra*.

"What have you done to yourself!" she exclaimed undaunted. Turning to the rest, she announced, "We were in college together. She was the topper in BSc. and went on to do M.Sc. and then Ph.D. in Physics."

"I later found Meta-physics more interesting," smiled Jeevanmoyee.

"Yes," said Mrs. Nath, "I had heard that you had taken voluntary retirement from Science College and become a *sannyasin* at Gangotri. I wrote to you, again and again, hoping that some letter or the other will reach. Come on, now that you are here, cure me of my ailment. Make me alright again."

Jeevanmoyee was silent.

"Please, for old time's sake!" said Mrs. Nath.

Jeevanmoyee kept quiet.

"You won't help?"

Anit could not keep back his own anger anymore..."You didn't help us either."

"Yes, you could have made Dinu live," Chandan too came out with his complaint. "You just turned Dinu back into a fossil."

"It was the best and only end for him," said Jeevanmoyee Ma. "There is an order in the way that The Supreme created life on earth. It should not be disturbed."

Yes, Anit remembered. None of the Jurassic Park films had got happy endings.

"The earth's history is divided into certain periods or eras. One succeeds another. One evolves from another. Both Western and Indian philosophers say so. Science can study it but not play with it. You tried to do that," Jeevanmoyee reproached Professor Chakladar. She also reproached herself.

"It had also been a mistake on my part to have given you the *mantra*-charged water. I had just been carried away by your passion, and moved by your sense of failure. But I had later realised that I had been wrong. I should not have given you the means of reviving what The Supreme Himself had brought to a closure. Activating an egg fossilized 65 million years ago! It was never meant to be."

"Teach me some of what you know, I pray," Houdini put in his own plea. "I have spent my life in the pursuit of magic. But I had never dreamt of this. Neither in Europe nor in America is there any magic equal to this."

There was a flash of anger in Jeevanmoyee Ma's eyes as she said: "Don't give this the name of 'magic'. This is ancient Ayurveda. India did master scientific principles that could turn living organisms into stone and then bring them back to life, and *vice versa*. But the world is not yet ready for them. Yes, it had indeed been a mistake on my part to give the pot of water to anyone, a mistake I will not make again."

She paused and looked at Mrs. Nath. "That is why I will not give you any miracle cure for your aches and pains. You are in a certain phase of life – just as I am – let us be content with that. The best we can do is to be happy as we are – with whatever we have got and even with whatever we have not."

"But we saw you sprinkle some water from your *lota* as you came into our place, and chant some *mantra*s as well? What were they for?"asked Mr. Nath.

"They were not for any physical ailment she had, but for her mental state. I remember the sprinter in her, but I also remember the cribber. Crib, crib, crib, she used to do in our college days. From her letters, I could make out that she hasn't changed at all."

"Yes, that's true," Mrs. Nath admitted. She narrated the whole story of how she drove Gaju to desperation. "My fault and I am trying to correct that," she said at the end.

"See, you haven't changed all that," Jeevanmoyee smiled. "You were always a sport and you are being a sport now in admitting your fault."

Gaju brought in *laddus*, fruits and nuts.

After just a few, Jeevanmoyee got up to go. "Don't leave," said Mrs. Nath. "At least stay the night?" But Jeevanmoyee left. She did not even take the lift that Baba offered to the railway station. They had to be content with just getting a taxi for her.

Further

In the next few days, everyone including Gaju had been told everything over and over again. No one could talk of anything else. Sanjay, Tarini and Ranjit, and schoolfellows from across the classes had dropped in. Padam too had come, so proud that he had a pet dog that had attacked a dinosaur.

Soon one evening, Paramjeet brought Professor Chakladar over to Anit's place for tea. Houdini too had come there and now the two of them had forgotten their Goa enmity. The Naths too had dropped in. As advised by Ma Jeevanmoyee, Mrs. Nath was making an effort to be up and about. She went across to the neighbours rather than lie in bed all day.

Ma brought in *samosas* and *chai* and Paramjeet served them round.

"I have something to ask," Houdini looked Professor Chakladar in the eye. "You are such a reputed man of science. Why did you give me a false name at Goa?"

"Because my peers – the fellow scientists – had ridiculed me so much. They had made me feel that what I was doing was not supported by either law or science, that it wasn't even research. But I had compounded some growth hormones together and needed subjects to try it upon – very much like rats and guinea pigs are needed for trying out a new serum. And my serum was successful – *you* know that. You have seen my Plesiosaur."

"Well, I can't certify that it *was* a Plesiosaur, but that other serum you had – I can vouch for. It almost crippled me and I see from your walk that it also crippled you."

Anit recalled that both of them had got pricks that had

almost paralysed them.

"Well, now your reputation will soar, Dr. Bhide-Chakladar," said Houdini. "We are all witnesses to your achievement."

The professor shook his head. "Laboratory analysis of the egg may be impossible or inconclusive. Besides, I cannot take credit for Jeevanmoyee Ma. It was the water sanctified by her that had done the trick. No scientific discovery of mine."

"There is a lot of science in Ayurveda, just as in magic," observed Houdini. "I too believe that," said the professor. "If only ancient practices could be woven into modern science, the world would see wonders."

"I found a change in you," said Houdini. "When you were trying to convert a duck into a Plesiosaur, you had no concern for the other ducks that would be eaten up in the process. You were bothered only about your own experiment, your own success. But this time you were keeping your amazing result to yourself. It was these kids and their teacher who broke into your privacy, and that journalist fellow who made it public. Why was that?"

"It must be Dinu's doing. You see, when I saw him peek out of that fossil, I saw a baby being born – just a baby–a newborn, although 65 million years old. Brachiosaurus, Barapasaurus, whatever he was, I felt love, I felt life. But that's all gone now. Dinu's gone."

He seemed to about to break down again and Anit was glad that the doorbell rang and Stickler came in.

It was a changed Stickler too, warm and informal with his arms outstretched. "I am so proud of you – and your friends – my school-kids all. You played a big role in this, as I came to know through Paramjeet and Jaydeep."

Neo too made his entry at this point, through the door that Anit had left open. "I say, wasn't it fun for you yesterday – the papers were full of it and the TV too."

"Sir, it wasn't exactly fun," Anit could not help saying. "Oh, I know," said Neo, immediately contrite. "It was so sad – the creature had to go back to being an egg —- but, wasn't it also fun? Overall?" He went forward to shake the professor's hand. "My congratulations on your fantastic find. No, no, my condolences for its deplorable demise."

"It is indeed a sad time for me," the professor said. "Now there is nothing left for me to do. And I have long left my teaching job." Anit looked at his shaggy, bent head and felt a lump rising in his throat.

Houdini brought out a letter from his pocket. "There doesn't seem much for me to do here either. My sister has written that her son has found a small opening for me in Patna. She has sent me a train ticket which is for tomorrow."

"You are too old now, Houdini, to be on the roads again, performing magic shows," said Mrs. Nath. "I noticed that you often put your hand on your chest. Do as Champa says. Well, what is the opening, anyway?"

"It is to teach simple magic tricks as at a hobby centre for children."

"Lucky children!" said Mrs. Nath. "I remember as a child how impressed I used to be by your magic tricks."

"Thanks, Meera, and thanks for giving me my name: Houdini. Well, I *will* do what my sister says. A lifetime gone after magic *will* end with magic, and now, *He He He He* ! I must do a vanishing trick."

"I will also make a move," said the professor. "No, Paramjeet, you don't have to drop me. I'll take a taxi."

A motorcycle roared outside. Jaydeep appeared at the door.

"A smuggling racket has been busted in Goa," he announced. "There are lava beds below the ground there and by the sea and there are lots of dinosaur fossils trapped in them. Some people had already discovered it and been smuggling the fossils out to private museums and laboratories in foreign countries. Now at long last the Goa government has found it out."

"So that is what was going below the old Portuguese fort!" exclaimed Houdini. "Those men were packing dinosaur fossils in secret, and employing a guard to keep people away from the site! Garuda's footprints, what a trick they had invented."

But Jaydeep had more to say.

"Now the Government will be in control of vast fossil beds connected across Maharashtra, Karnataka, and the Deccan in general. The fossils will stay on in India and a team of Indian scientists will be working on them. What is more, the Science Society has elected Professor Chakladar to be the leader of the team. He can have all the material, all the equipment, and all the freedom to do his research. The decision has just been made and will reach him by tomorrow."

Then Stickler thumped the professor on the back. He seemed no longer to be a stickler for proprieties.

"How do you know this?" asked the professor, looking both dazed and disbelieving.

"I am a journalist, Sir," said Jaydeep. "It's my job. Now, will you forgive me for whatever I did to your Dinu?"

Everybody dispersed happily. The house became quiet. Anit was feeling a bit low. The last few weeks had been action-packed. Now would it be dull and dreary? Would their team ABCD ever again have any adventures? Would it at least hang together in problems big and small? Or fall apart with time? What would the future hold?

He began to change for the bed, that is, get into the *kurta-pajamas* Dadi had brought and which he now used as sleeping-suits. Something brushed against his chest. It was the talisman – all but forgotten nowadays. Anit felt new energy flowing into him – as if Karna was asking him to boldly face whatever the future brought.

Epilogue: Waiting Again

The egg lay in the glass case of the National Museum. Because of its story, it was the entry or exhibit that every visitor made it a point to see.

The egg wondered if its story would have a replay, if someone would ever bring it to life again. Perhaps centuries later or even millennia. The earth will be even more changed then, with the glaciers all melted and contemporary civilization in ruins. A new species would rule the world, far advanced human beings who have developed super-powers from modern research. Someone or the other from that species would take the egg out of its glass case and free the force within. There would be some ferns and fronds on earth still left to feed upon. And the children of those times, like those known so briefly this time, would welcome him into their world.

Would it be like that? The egg knew it would. It just had to wait.